DEADLY DROPPINGS

WILLIAM LEROY

mossikpress@mail.com

Library of Congress Cataloguing-in-Publication Data

LeRoy, William [1.17.2023]

Deadly Droppings: A Maximo Morgan Mystery
by William LeRoy

p. cm
ISBN 979-8-9869494-2-0

1. Humor—Fiction.
2. Oklahoma, United States—Fiction.
3. Pidgeons—Fiction.
4. Mystery—Fiction.
I. Title

10 9 8 7 6 5 4 3 2 1

Manufactured in the United States of America
First Edition

DEADLY DROPPINGS

WILLIAM LEROY

TUESDAY
April 12, 2022

CHAPTER ONE

Max sat at his workstation inside Mister Quickie's copy shop, leaning back in his chair. Two desk plaques—one identifying him as "Maximo Morgan" by name, the other identifying his game as "Private Investigations"—were pushed aside to make room for his feet. He was off-duty, taking a break from both gumshoeing and Notary Public service he provided to copy shop customers in return for Quickie letting him occupy the space. For the past twenty minutes, he had been swapping war stories with Bill Crowe, a former brother-in-arms seated across the desk.

Crowe, about ten years younger, had briefly trained under him as a raw recruit and was still doing his bit, though no longer in the field. Both had seen a lot of action. Both had experienced multiple close calls. Both had plenty of breeze to shoot.

"Yeah, it was a German Schnauzer running wild on Northeast 4th Street that had my name on it," Crowe was saying, with another twitch of head and shoulder. "Sumbitch ambushed me; got hold of an ankle; took me off the front line for good. Just like the Krauts almost did to G.I. Joe."

G.I. Joe? Max drew a blank.

"Served in the armed forces branch, Max. Way before our time. Made countless deliveries through harm's way, including a twenty-mile dash during World War II with a message that saved hundreds of Italian civilians and allied troops from friendly American fire. His body is stuffed and mounted at Fort Monmouth in New, Jersey."

Stuffed and mounted? Max was impressed.

"Yeah, the services took care of their shell shocked veterans back in the day," his old buddy continued, with another twitch. "G.I. Joe was my old man's hero, and mine too. He's the reason I volunteered, along with the perks. Chicks go for guys in uniform."

Max recalled that Crowe had always been a chick magnet, and a playboy even as a married guy with kids. Though now dressed in civvies, he still had a full head of wavy red hair; and probably still had a furry chest. From the neck down, Max's pear-shaped physique had always been bare as a baby's bottom. His head had never produced more than what looked like fuzzy duckling feathers.

"You got out just in time, Max," said Bill. "Used to be that a mailman had time to get to know the civilians on his route—chicks go for guys who 'deliver'—but not anymore. Hell's bells, at my current headquarters posting all I have time to do is give the wink to suckers who come in after getting notice of registered mail, and maybe shout a few words of warning. Some poor saps don't know that registered mail is a trick used by the government to prove you got notice of the trouble you're in."

Crowe paused to put another stick of chewing gum into his gabber.

Max seized the opportunity to tell one of his own post-postal war stories.

As a kid he too had been inspired by his own old man's hero: Mike Hammer, a private dick back in the *Noir* days of the 1950s. After discovering his deceased father's attic stash of lurid pulp case reports as a teenager, he had devoured all the accounts of Hammer's hardboiled exploits written up by a guy named Mickey Spillane—from *I, The Jury* to *My Gun is Quick* to *Kiss Me, Deadly* and so on—which had led him to also study the cases worked by other famous gumshoes: Phillip Marlowe, Lew Archer, Travis McGee and those who came later, including even Jessica Fletcher.

"Mastering the musty books is a must for cutting the mustard in the gumshoe game," he said, "but just as important was my hands-on experience of serving in the postal service.

"As you yourself would well know, Bill, a mailman walking a route for twelve-plus years will occasionally spot a bent iron—that's private dick lingo for a stolen vehicle—or see a recipient of disability checks lifting an anvil in her driveway, maybe a tomcat sneaking out the back door of a married dame's house. During another twelve-plus years in the post office sorting room a would-be shamus gets opportunities to peek into barely sealed scented envelopes, carelessly wrapped plain brown paper packages; and inspect letters marked 'Personal & Confidential' that might have criminal content."

Max noticed that his buddy was looking at his watch, and twitching more spasmodicaly.

"Still, Yours Truly would not be where I am today if not for getting lucky and stumbling onto the record of my own personal hero, namely Brad Runyon a/k/a The Fat Mannn," he reported in his role model's baritone drawl that he had mastered. "Now there was a guy who deserved to be stuffed and mounted."

Runyon was a gumshoe back in the *Noir*, he explained, and personally delivered weekly case reports on the radio. Thankfully, eleven of the first-person accounts had been saved for posterity, and he had scored a set of CDs that had them all. Each began with the sound of heavy footsteps and the voice of a woman saying: *There he goes, into that drugstore. He's stepping on a set of scales.* Following sounds of a coin dropping and a machine spitting out a card, the dame would say: *Weight: two-hundred and forty-six pounds. Fortune: danger! Whooo is it?*

"The Fat Mannn," Max again drawled, as his one-man audience—obviously listening carefully—stared up at the ceiling and sighed.

"So yeah, finally a hero I could live up to," he continued. "Overweight, but light on his feet, and a good dancer. Middle-aged but hip to the scene. Unflappable when caught in tight spots, with a knack for unraveling cases of murrrderrr. Based on a photo that went with the CD of Runyon's recorded case reports, I outfitted myself in this vintage double-breasted suit and those two-tone shoes like my hero wore. I laid my mitts on a realistic copy of the .45 gat Runyon packed in a shoulder holster. I set up shop here at Mister Quickie's, and bingo, a skirt ankled up to the desk.

"Not your ordinary bran muffin; a real cupcake…" Barely into laying out the details of *Case of a Jealous Strawberry-Blonde*, Max noticed that his former brother-in-arms—still staring up at the ceiling—was now moving his lips as though silently counting.

"Ordinarily I'm a ham-and-eggs guy before lunch, but there was something about this dame that made my mouth waterrr. She batted her baby blues and…"

Crowe lunged forward. In a hushed tone of voice: "Now that you mention it, Max, old pal, I myself happen to be faced with a…with a matter that needs to be privately investigated."

His old postal service buddy, not seen or heard from for at least five years, went on to confide that since the German Schnauzer attack, he had been suffering from a condition called PTSD, but getting no TLC from the USPS. He admitted he had been bucking for a Section 8 Psycho Discharge with full pension, but…

"Ever hear of an old TV show called *M*A*S*H* about a military mail clerk named Klinger during the Korean War?" Crowe asked, before again pausing to start unwrapping another stick of gum. "I scored a box set of DVDs and studied Klinger's moves, but…"

After putting the chewing gum into his pie hole—which seemed to calm the twitching—the veteran mailman confessed to showing up for work dressed as a dame, one time as a nun; to forging threatening letters to himself from obviously insane postal customers; to attempting to bribe his superior officer. He copped to joining a right wing militia and wearing a Nazi helmet on duty for awhile. He stowed away in a mail bag, naked, and had himself delivered to his superior officer's wife on Valentine's Day. He torched an entire truckload of heavy *Restoration Hardware* catalogues, but…

"For that trick, thanks to the damn union rep, I got a commendation medal and USPS Employee of the Month certificate, but no medical discharge and no pension."

Max understood where his old buddy was coming from. "Don't worry, old buddy," he said. "I myself once went through a rough patch, literally, while delivering a load…"

"I can't take it anymore, Max. I need permanent R & R. But Homer…I raised and trained him to be my ticket out from under the stress of postal service, but…"

Up from his chair, pacing back and forth in front of the desk, Bill Crowe wailed that a young Homer, his "pride-and-joy", had "flown the coop". Though not recalling Bill's kids by name, Max remembered him boasting about a "chip off the old block" who by now would be a teenager.

"I have looked all over the county for him," said the obviously worried old block. "He may have gotten into harm's way, but I have a hunch Homer has been…I don't want to ruffle any feathers by personally pointing a crooked finger, but I have reason to think Homer has, let's say, fallen into bad company."

Only a missing juvenile delinquent case, but…Gumshoeing opportunities had been scarce as proverbial hens' teeth for weeks.

"It's a delicate matter, Max; not the kind of thing I would want real cops sticking their noses into," Bill said, understandably. The local Barney Fifes were blind as proverbial bats. "And no doubt all the other private detectives in town would charge an arm-and-leg to help a guy they don't even know, but…"

Max took his feet off the desk and sat up straight. Thankfully, there were no other private dicks operating in the small town of Henryetta, Oklahoma. But a yardbird based in the nearby county seat town of Okmulgee had recently put a face, name, telephone number and slogan — *Tom Owsley Sleeps With One Eye Open* — on local billboards and benches.

"And time is running out. Homer is entered in a big FFF event that scouts will be watching, and needs to report by day after tomorrow at the latest. If I don't find him…Say, Maxie," said Crowe after stopping in his tracks, "why don't you drop by the VFW tonight. We'll dip our beaks in the punch bowl like old times. I'll check out the chicks while you check out the FFF member most likely involved in leading Homer astray."

Max had never dipped his beak in a punch bowl with Bill Crowe, nor with anyone else. But once a mailman, always a mailman, bound by a shared oath that neither rain, nor snow, nor gloom of night would keep him from an appointed task.

CHAPTER TWO

As an also almost middle-aged woman from a neighboring farm continued to chatter like a magpie about the so-called private lives of the Kardashians, "Coo" Haggard went about putting the finishing touches to the customer's cut-and-dye job. In addition to handling a full load of household chores, Coo—thankfully childless—worked some mornings as a hairdresser in order to financially support her passion for pigeon racing.

Not least among the joys of her so-called hobby was its annoyance to her husband, Gary Lee "Big Bert" Haggard, whose passion was for killing winged creatures of every feather. Not that Bert was locally unusual in that regard. The bloodthirsty notion that fowl were fair game was inbred among most males in Okmulgee County. Her own father, for instance, had named her in honor of Alice Cooper because the famous old shock rocker was reported to have bitten off the head of a live chicken and drunk its blood during an onstage performance.

Country and small town boys who came along later had picked up on the possibly urban legend dating back to her father's "good old days", and tried to woo her by…Despite herself, a verse from a different singer's song that Bert called "their song" began to run through Coo's mind:

♫*She don't like her eggs all runny/ She thinks crossin' her legs is funny/ She's my baby, I'm her honey/ I'm never gonna let her go…* ♫ She hated men.

"Not all men, it seems," said her customer, Clara Lindsey, a notorious gossip. "Some say there has recently been quite a lot of unfeathered 'Billing-and-Cooing' in your 'La Maison Derriere' loft."

Realizing she had muttered aloud her general sentiment, "I was referring to the likes of Kanye, who has treated Kim so shabbily," Coo cooly replied. "But now that you mention it, Clara, yes, I have been trying to breed one of of my hens with one of Bill Crowe's cocks," she said, which happened to be true, though unbeknownst to Bill.

"Your hen and his cock: my, my. Well then, that explains why Bill has been seen, uh, visiting so often while Big Bert is always down on your south forty, growing weeds without a license, people say. Though it is odd that you two pigeon fanciers would be, uh,' breeding', seeing as how you and Bill are known to be bitter racing rivals."

That too was true. Bill Crowe and she were bitter racing competitors, and then some, which was the reason she had stooped to flirting with the incorrigible womanizer, who happened to be Bert's oldest and only friend. The Dixie Classic—otherwise known as the Grand Prix of southern pigeon racing—was scheduled for Friday. And she was determined to secretly undo the unfair advantage her rival's prize cock would have over her prize hen by his admittedly masterful use of the so-called widowhood technique of pre-race training.

"Bill drives a mail truck to Oklahoma City once or twice a week," she further explained. "From there he releases both his and my pigeons for ninety-mile homeward training flights. And this farm is almost exactly ten miles from town," she continued. "So on other days Bill has been bringing his cocks to me and taking my hens to his in-town loft. We each release the birds the next morning in order for them to have a long enough sprint home to stay in shape for the Grand Prix."

Bill's so-called widowhood technique was designed to encourage flirtatious "billing-and-cooing" between his prize racing pigeon and a given hen for days preceding a race, but deny his horny homer satisfaction of consummating a conjugal relationship. Simultaneously, he would introduce a rival cock onto the scene. Driven by lust and possessive male jealousy, Homer, when released from a distant starting point, would fly home as if with wings of an eagle.

"Bill's prize cock is one of the favorites in at least the Oklahoma bracket of this year's Dixie Classic," she added, while also adding a bit more shine to her nosy customer's hairdo. "So the joint training exercises also give me an opportunity to scout the competition. As they say, Clara, 'Keep your friends close, and your enemies closer.'"

"Yes, I have heard about the, uh, 'trophies' won by Bill Crowe's 'prize cock'."

The so-called widowhood technique did not work to motivate hens such as Coo exclusively raced, which was why she had so far never won the Grand Prix prize money that would allow her to finally take flight from her miserable marriage. This year, however, she had good reason to hope things would be different.

Based on the same sexist principle underlying the widowhood technique—"Women Weaken Wings"—she had held onto Bill Crowe's prize cock for days, during which time one of her hens—an insatiable breeder named Lurleen Lumpkin—had sated Homer with billing, cooing, and then some. As a result of her "Honeymoon" training technique, while her prize female competitor—Princess Kasmir—would be in fine feather for Friday's race, her main local opponent would be barely able to…

"And Bill and Big Bert have been such close friends since all the way back to grade school," Clara clucked. "You would think they would make a point to visit with one another during Bill's, uh, cock deliveries."

"No doubt they would enjoy dressing up as so-called 'Paul Revere Minutemen' and shooting off their mouths and muskets more often," said Coo, tiring of the verbal fencing. "But I won't allow it. Bert and I have reached a hard-fought understanding about…"

"Ah, I see."

"Good," said Coo, yanking the beauty parlor smock off her prying customer. "The slightly iridescent sheen of your purple-

and-blue hairdo gives you the look of a Jewel Pigeon, and it's almost time Bert is allowed to release his new second-best friend, Donald. So you may need a sharp eye on your way to…"

"Donald?" said Clara Lindsey, with a start. "Is 'Donald' one of those ferocious penned-up bird dogs that tried to attack me on my way in?"

"Oh no, my dear. Bert's new hunting accomplice is far more dangerous than…"

Speak of the devil, her hubby, all six-foot four-inches of ugly menace, appeared in the doorway, holding a hand behind his back.

"You're running late, Honey," he said with his trademark shit-eating smirk, "which gave me and Donald a chance to get something for you," he said, taking his hand from behind him and holding out…

Oh no. Coo lunged at the brute, but…He snatched back his gloved claw that held…

"Don't worry, Baby, it's just a turtle dove, not your precious Princess Kashmir, and she's still alive," he said, before…

To Coo's horror, the grisly beast put the dove's head into his mouth and, as he chewed feathers and all… "Wanna go into the bedroom to 'bill and coo'?"

♫*In spite of ourselves/ We're gonna spite our noses/ right off of our faces/ I'm never gonna let her go. . .* ♫

CHAPTER THREE

At home for lunch at his mom's kitchen table, Max chewed on *Case of a Runaway Juvenile Delinquent* while finishing off a fried chicken. Yeah, the case was only a bush league gig, but according to a recent piece in *Gumshoe Gazette*, tracking down runaways had been private dick bread-and-butter since back in days of *Noir*.

The trade magazine article had featured a run-down of the career of a Black gumshoe out in L.A.—Sam Marlowe— who made a name for himself by bringing runaway dames back to the nests of movie stars named Clark Gable and Charles Chaplin. Yeah, the truants were skirts and likely not teenagers, but Dashiell Hammett—the guy who wrote up Sam Spade's cases—and Raymond Chandler—who scribed for Phillip Marlowe—had reportedly relied on Sam Marlowe for tips on private dick know-how and lingo that they must have passed on to the shamuses they wrote about.

In other words, finding Bill Crowe's boy, Homer, would sharpen his game for frying bigger fish, such as girlfriends and wives on the lam.

"Max, I don't like it," said his mom. "The main reason teenagers run away is that they are unhappy at home, which is why your father—may he rest in peace—thought it was my fault that you kept coming back from where he dropped you. And I never approved of you hanging out at the post office with that Bill Crowe, who has a bad reputation for being a womanizer. A man who would cheat at marriage, would cheat at anything.

"Bill can't help being a chick magnet," Max explained. "He was born with wavy red hair that naturally looks like a duck tail on the back of his head."

"Yet he marches in 4th of July parades dressed up as a Reverend and…"

Reverend?

"One of those Paul Revere 'Midnight Riders' who go out into the countryside and, from what I hear, shoot ducks with shotguns just for fun," said Mom, taking away his plate before he had gotten to the gizzard. "A man who would do such a thing to our fine feathered friends is not fit to be parent of a teenaged boy."

To avoid more argument, Max got up from the table, ankled out the back door, got into his mom's brown Buick boiler and headed back to his Mr. Quickie workstation.

Mom's already low opinion of men with wandering eyes had hit rock bottom after she was left in a Downward Dog condition by a yoga instructor, Maharishi Archie, who ran off with another student named Fatima, who could do not only a Bird of Paradise pose but also a trick called One-Legged Pigeon. He himself had no beef with his mom's attitude toward so-called ladies men in general, but Bill Crowe was a brother-in-arms suffering from PMS and…Truth be told, Max was under pressure to work a case that could be written up as a book like an *Adventure of Sherlock Holmes*.

His own "Watson" was a teenaged kid, a wannabe P.I. who looked up to him as an also overweight role model. After hanging around his desk, jotting notes as he listened and learned, the kid had sent a case report to a book publisher—titled *Case of a Puzzling Book*—and…

Sure enough, the kid's three-wheeled bicycle with over-sized seat was parked on the sidewalk in front of Mr. Quickie's.

Out of the boiler and into the copy shop, again sure enough, a chair set beside his desk was occupied by the pesky kid.

"Gee, Mr. Maximo," said his case jotter, "Mr. Quickie's assistant saw you leave for lunch at eleven-fifteen. It's now past two o'clock and I…I mean we are up against a deadline."

"Working a new case," said Max after sitting down. "Took on the lay this morning and had to, uh, digest what went down."

"Finally," said the kid, taking a pencil from behind a stuck-out ear and a small spiral-bound notebook from a shirt pocket. "The big cheese at Mossik Press says *Case of a Puzzling Book* won't make it onto a bestseller list until readers see that it's part of a series. 'Publish or Perish' is the name of the game."

Dog-gone-it, the price set by the publisher was the problem. At $7.99 a pop, not even Mom had sprung for a copy of the book. The only deadline he cared about was finding Bill Crowe's young Homer by Thursday before a big FFF event.

"So, what's afoot, Mr. Maximo? A case of murrrderrr, by any chance?"

"No such luck, at least not yet. All I have doped out so far is that a local teenaged male has run away from home, and…"

"Runaway teenager?" said the kid, putting the pencil and notebook back to rest. "That's common as pigeon poop around here, Mr. Maximo. I may be the only teenager in town who has not run away from home, at least not yet."

"Listen and learn, kid. If you are ever gonna walk-the-walk in gumshoes, you're gonna have to figure out how to take one step at a time," Max advised. "This case gives you a chance to get off your backside and do something besides jot details of cases to be written up, starting here and now. Ever cross paths with a kid named Homer Crowe? Outstanding, well trained athlete. Potential big league bonus baby who…"

"There's a kid in my class we call Homer Simpson, but he's no athlete, and…No; no one currently in junior high school is named Homer Crowe, not that I know of."

"See; that's evidence. The runaway kid must be a senior high school drop-out who has taken his eye off the ball and focused it on girls, a sure sign he's headed for trouble. Keep listening and learning, kid. Your next step is to…"

"Actually, Mr. Maximo, I don't think I will have time to work this, uh, case," said the uppity trainee, rising from his chair like a yeasty half-baked dinner roll.

No time? Ha! Max himself had once been a pear-shaped, flat-footed teenager without aptitude for any ordinary extra-curricular activity. Like his youthful self, the kid no doubt had nothing to do except…

"Looks like you're not wise to the prequel to *Case of The Maltese Falcon* that recently came out," he said to the young wannabe private dick, who claimed Sam Spade had been his original role model.

"Prequel?"

"Yeah, a case report called *Spade & Archer* chronicles a lay Spade was working when he first moved to San Fran, before he hit the bigtime."

"Oh yeah?" said the kid, re-parking his big butt in the chair. "What was in play, murder?"

"Not necessarily. At the time the *femme fatale* supposedly named 'Ruth Wonderly' ankled into Spade's office and hired him to recover that priceless bird statue—listen and learn, kid—Sam was working a case for a rich banker; tracking down the client's ne'er-do-well son, a runaway teenager."

"And?" said the kid, again poised to jot.

"That's how the gumshoe game works," Max impatiently explained. "To pay the bills and stay sharp, a private dick feeds on small game until a proverbial 'Golden Goose' waddles into the office."

"Oh," said the kid, again putting away pencil-and-paper; and again standing. "I hope you don't mind, Mr. Maximo," he said, extending a pudgy hand for a shake. "It's just that Mr. Owsley up in Okmulgee has offered me a chance to be his local bird dog, and…"

Owsley? The yardbird who had recently put pictures of his big fat winking face on every billboard and bench in the county? The guy who supposedly slept with one private eye open? The kid was dumping Yours Truly for a chance to drum up cases for a no doubt armchair P.I. who didn't know wet-from-windy about gumshoeing?

"Mr. Owsley worked for twenty years as an OSBI agent," said the smartass kid, referring to the Oklahoma State Bureau of Investigation. "He has his own eavesdropping equipment, plus all kinds of other high-tech gadgets for sleuthing. He is already working a big case of some kind, but wants me to be both his spotter for new lays and no doubt his case reporter. You know, like Archie Goodwin did for Mr. Nero Wolfe back in the *Noir*."

Though staggered by the kid's low blow to the chops, Max began to mentally bob-and-weave. Brad Runyon had never needed a jotter; the original Fat Man reported his own cases by word of mouth on the radio. And hmmm… He'd heard audio was back to the bigtime in the form of a new technique called podcasting. In other words, good riddance to his jotting "Watson". To hell with overpriced books that nobody could afford to hold in their mitts and read.

CHAPTER FOUR

Printed in red on Dorothy "Dodo" Vogel's business cards were the words *Hopeless Romantic*. And to Dodo nothing signified hopeless romance more dramatically than marriage, which was why her business cards were also emblazoned with her job description, *Wedding Planner*. But as some famous person famously said, the course of true love never ran smoothly, which was the reason she was now engaged in yet another tedious meeting with yet another mother of yet another bride-to-be about the hopelessly unromantic subject of "budget".

Due to the hurry-up nature of pending nuptials, she had already crossed-off *Save-the-Date Notices*, *Announcements* and *Invitations* from her checklist.

In order to qualify for the One-Night Stand honeymoon rate at the local Fountainblue Motel, she had made arrangements for a mid-week ceremony, 4:00 p.m. to 4:15 p.m. in the employee lounge of the local G&H Decoy Company—home of the world famous "Henryettan" goose decoy—where both bride and groom worked.

There would be no catered reception, no cake, no champagne. Only donuts and sodas from a canteen machine would be available to guests during rites of matrimony officiated by a part-time Justice of the Peace.

And yet the client's mother, a Ms. Ruby Keller, continued to fret about expenses incidental to making her daughter's wedding the most special event of their lives.

"It's just that, well, this is not Kandi's first most special event of our lives," said the penny-pinching mother of the bride-to-be. "And her soon-to-be ex is still dickering about…"

"Did you say soon-<u>to-be</u> ex?"

"Wayne 'Deal-a-Day' Dean is a used car salesman, but not a complete fool. He either signs the paper tomorrow, or we walk."

"The course of true love never runs smoothly, but is always worth the trip," Dodo advised. "I myself have walked down the aisle three times. Each stroll was more special than the one before."

"But wouldn't Kandi's freshly washed-and-ironed denim outfit be more suitable? She will be coming straight from the company paint line, without time to change before or after. And my daughter is not exactly a virgin bride. Little Deal-a-Day will be again present, this time out of the womb and standing right there as best man."

"May I remind you, Ruby, that I am happily providing my own white satin wedding dress for the occasion, for only a modest additional fee to cover costs of handling, cleaning and re-handling. A wedding, after all, is nothing if not a photo op. And rest assured…"

"Photos? How much will pictures cost?"

"I myself will photographically record the event, and my teenaged son, Butch Junior, will tend to the boom box that will play a selection of appropriate music. All as part of my bargain Semi-Elopement Package. Not a day goes by that I myself do not… Well, here," said Dodo, handing to the client a photo album memorializing one of her own weddings. "Regardless of what the future may hold for Kandi and What's-His-Name—the course of true love never runs smoothly—just imagine the joy you and your daughter will have someday, looking back on, uh, one of the most special days of your lives."

As the mother of the bride-to-be began to thumb through the album, Dodo indulged in a mournful sigh signifying what were said to be the saddest words of tongue or pen: "what might have been". Missing from all three of her wedding albums—except for a single photobomb—was memorialization of her one true love.

Billy Crowe was the drum major for the high school band; usually outfitted in a gold-braided uniform and cap with a feathery plume. And her date at the Sadie Hawkins Day Dance. Afterward, quite out of uniform…Well. the next morning, in keeping with mutual promises of everlasting love made in the back seat of a school bus, she had rushed to the local *Shotgun Sally Bridal Salon* and…

"Gee, Ms. Vogel," said the current bride-to-be, coming from a bedroom; wearing the very same dress she had picked up from layaway at *Shotgun Sally's* almost twenty years ago, "it's awful skimpy."

"Nonsense, my dear. Mini-skirts are still the rage for formal occasions."

"For crying out loud," said the mother of the bride-to-be, "there's no need to advertise Kandi's, uh, condition."

"The bare midriff is not only stylish, but practical," Dodo explained. "Alterations to your own, uh, old-fashioned brown wedding dress would have been expensive."

"But the tattoo of my ex's name next to my belly-button shows," the bride-to-be wailed. "Grady wouldn't like that."

"A minor detail, easily and inexpensively fixed with a splash of make-up."

"I still say your denim outfit…"

"No, Mommy! I want a white dress to match the doves, and this one is still almost white."

"Doves? What doves?"

"Well, yes, a release of doves could be arranged," said Dodo, before going on to explain the many complications involved. Domesticated doves, while said to mate for life and therefore supposedly signifying marital stability, were utterly lacking in survival instincts and more often than not signified early abandonment when ceremoniously released into the wild.

"Do you not recall the tragic incident at the Vatican eight or nine years ago," she said, before going on to describe the gory details of the ill advised release of two doves by children standing beside Pope Francis. Intended to signify setting wings to the

Pope's prayer for peace in Ukraine, the ceremony was marred when the defenseless birds were set upon and ravaged by crows. Nevertheless…

"If Kandi is set on a feathered feature, let's see: sacrifice of, say, two white doves to celebrate the nuptials—in addition to possibly signifying doom—would cost…"

"No birds!" the mother of the bride-to-be declared.

"Aw, Mommy," the bride-to-be wailed.

"For a modest additional fee, I could arrange a release of Butch Junior's flock of pigeons," Dodo offered. "Unlike doves…"

"Pigeons! I don't want ordinary pigeons. They're not white. They will eat all the souvenir rice and…"

Dodo explained that because members of her teenaged son's flock were no doubt blessed with the homing instincts for which pigeons were famous, they would safely return to their coop following a ceremonial release, signifying steadfastness to a domesticated condition. "Though not feathered white, their bluish plumage would add a complementary contrast to the almost still white…"

"Bluish gray pigeons would match your denim outfit, Kandi!"

"Aw, Mommy. Pigeons poop."

"Not if we eliminated the rice."

"Well, I can't guarantee…"

"I'll pay for one or the other—rental of the white dress or the pigeons—but not both," the mother of the bride-to-be declared in no uncertain terms.

"Yes, I quite agree," said Dodo with a sigh. Though said by some to be an omen of good luck dating back to the no doubt long-and-happy marriage of Mark Anthony and Elizabeth Taylor, to her—a hopeless romantic—pigeons pooping on the keepsake wedding dress would painfully signify the unromantic ordeal of being jilted almost twenty years ago—almost at the altar—by Billy Crowe.

CHAPTER FIVE

Max got up from the kitchen table and again promised his mom he would not drink punch at an FFF meeting. He did not promise he would not throw a punch or two. Yeah, a few feathers might fly at the VFW, where Bill Crowe would finger the joker he suspected of leading young Homer astray. When all was said and done, the chip off Bill's old block would be safely back home. And so would he; likely not later than nine o'clock, he again promised, before ankling out the back door and getting behind the wheel of the brown boiler.

Mom was anxious about a tomorrow morning appointment with a doctor in Oklahoma City, which was understandable. It was because of a feet condition medics called metatarsus adductus that she had been put on the back row of yoga class. But since then she had started keeping company with a gentleman friend and—though Maharishi Archie had closed his *Proud Peacock Studio* before running of with a teacher's pet—his mom had decided to spring for a pair of orthopedic shoes previously recommended by a fancy-pants big-city sawbones.

Max had his doubts about Dr. Pfau, who was a dame and pricey. He himself had once gone to her for help, and while his own condition—called femoral retroversion or "duck feet"—was the exact opposite of his mom's in-toed affliction, the doc's recommended treatment had been suspiciously the same. "Connecting to Mother Earth's core allows us to spiritually connect to our individual cores," the doc had repeatedly said. "And my own patented brand of footwear is both stylish and affordable."

He didn't buy it. Embedding magnets into soles of shoes to fix falling arches was bassackward science to his way of thinking, but…"The sole is gateway to the soul," his mom had said during supper, repeating one of Dr. Pfau's slogans. "If only I had bought a pair of stylish but affordable *Magno Mocs* before…before I flunked yoga," she'd added with a sigh.

Arriving at an ordinary house that served as the town's VFW Hall, Max himself was a little anxious. Ordinarily, he would have been proud to attend a meeting of the FFF, no doubt an organization of veterans from other branches of service involved in sponsoring youth sports, but…Dog-gone-it, he had been unable to fit into the pants, shirt and jacket of his old USPS uniform. And though wearable, his cap—adorned with an outdated insignia depicting an eagle poised for flight—had become uncomfortably tight and unattractively high-riding.

After ankling to the hall's front door, he took a deep breath. Inside…Max exhaled a sigh of relief.

None of the three-dozen or so FFF members gathered in a largish living-and-dining-room-size space were in uniform. At least not exactly. A red-bearded guy sticking out a beefy hand for a shake was wearing only a baseball-style cap, adorned with a sewn-on patch depicting not a US Postal Service eagle poised for flight, but only the words DUCKS UNLIMITED above an image of what looked to be a fowl of some kind falling from the sky.

"Benny Ward," the guy said, shaking his mitt. "Don't believe I've had the pleasure. Are you a Wandering Warbler Watcher?"

"Maximo Morgan's the name. And, uh, yeah, you could say watching is my game."

"Righto. To each his own, I say. We're all Fine Feathered Friends tonight."

Max felt a tug at his elbow. He turned around and, "Don't waste your time on Buckshot Benny," Bill Crowe whispered, before leading him away from the "fine feathered friend" at the door. "Benny is one of us. The FFF member most likely messing with Homer is that hot chick standing over there by the punch bowl."

Hmmm.

He had heard of individual members of youth sports organizations feathering their own nests by recruiting—and exploiting—big league prospects to come under their personal wings, but was surprised that the fingered suspect in Homer Crowe's case would be a broad.

The client again referred to the lay as a "delicate matter". He didn't want to go off half-cocked and ruin a "good thing he had going". He didn't dare even talk to the suspect, much less confront her and risk "putting a cat among pigeons". At least not yet; not until Max, his "bird dog", had flushed the "hen" into the open.

"Her name is Coo Haggard," said Bill, with a nod of head toward the bluish-haired dame now dipping her beak into a cup. "The big guy standing next to her and watching like a hawk is her husband. I'll decoy him, so you can move in on her, but don't mention my name and be careful what you say. My wife is around here somewhere, with that security pet of hers. Cassandra can hear a pin drop and repeats everything she hears. You can't miss her; she's a flaming redhead."

Bill headed for the door, waving what looked to be a pint bottle of hooch at the suspect's tall husband, who took the bait and followed. Max ankled toward the suspect, but…"Aren't you the Notary Public stamper who works on private investigations for Mr. Quickie," said an easy-on-the-eyes blonde, sidling up beside him. "Friend of Bill's or…?"

"Old postal service buddies," said Max, with a casual one-finger salute to the bill of his cap.

"Oh, too bad; I thought you might be here on a 'domestic' investigation," the dame said, with a glance toward a dark-haired tall job who had a redheaded parrot perched on her shoulder. "I am also, well, not an old but a longtime friend of Bill's. Not that my attendance here tonight signifies anything still hopelessly romantic between us. My son, Butch Junior, is a pigeon fancier.

"I like your cap," she said, moving closer, batting her baby blues, and handing him a letter-size brochure along with a business card that identified her as a hopelessly romantic wedding planner. "I'll be on the chartered bus to the World of Wings Adventure on Sunday. If you're interested in adventure, I'll save a seat for you, between me and Butch Junior."

Max went back to ankling toward the dame named Coo Haggard. At the punch bowl, before he could make a play… "Deliver the 'mail' and be quick about it," the suspect hissed.

"Sorry to disappoint you, Sister," he answered, with another one-finger salute. "I'm now retired from postal service and…"

"My mistake. I saw you talking to Bill, and assumed you were, uh, standing in for Homer."

"Yeah, as a matter of fact, young Homer <u>has</u> gone missing, now that you mention it."

In answer to his cagy grilling, the suspect copped to holding Bill's pride-and-joy under her wing for a few days, but only for "treatment". Young Homer had become infested with lice, she claimed, not by any of her girls.

"Hygiene is a *Maison Derriere* hallmark. Homer was in fine feather when I released him."

As he moved in on the suspect, intending to turn up the heat to a third degree… **"Hear ye! Hear ye!"** someone hollered.

Max wheeled around. At one end of the room an old codger had got up onto a box, holding a bullhorn up to his face. **"This here meeting of the Fine Feathered Friends of Okmulgee County is now called to order!"**

The old coot went on to announce that a truck for "Dixie Classic contestants" would be parked in the high school lot for loading between noon and 2:00 p.m. on Thursday. A "release" was scheduled for 6:00 a.m. on Friday from Birmingham, Alabama, which was five hundred and forty miles from Henryetta as a crow flew, he added. For those who did not feel obliged to personally welcome home racers, there would be a watch party at the town hall for remote tracking of electronically registered finishers, starting at five o'clock.

"**As you all know, Bill Crowe's prize cock and Coo Haggard's equally prize entry will be up against each other again…**"

"Bill's cock up against Coo's entry again," someone squawked.

"**…but whether Bill's bird or Coo's makes the best time…**"

"Bill and Coo making time."

"Don't forget Skeeter Swinford's cock, Bandit!"

"**…whether it's Homer or Princess Kasmir that gets home first…**"

"Bill and Coo. Bill and Coo."

"Keep your eye on Bandit to make history!"

"**…whether we race 'em, shoot 'em, eat 'em or just watch 'em, let's remember: we are all Fine Feathered Friends!**

"**Which reminds me. The Governor will be passing trough town on race day…**"

Booooo…

"**…so to all you hunters and Reverends, no guns allowed!**"

Boooooooooso…

"**Turn on the boom box, Mildred!**"

Music began to play and…Hmmm. Max had an inkling of a hunch that *Case of a Runaway Juvenile Delinquent* was turning out to be…

"I've saved the first dance just for you, soldier," said the hopelessly romantic blonde wedding planner, suddenly swooped down beside him and taking his hand in hers.

♫**People may smile, but I don't mind/ They'll never understand the kind of fun I find…**♫

FFF members began to stomp their feet, and…

♫**Doin' the pigeon (coo) (coo)…**♫

…then kick one foot behind them…

♫**Doin' the pigeon (coo) (coo)…**♫

…bobbing their heads back and forth like…

♫**Doin the pigeon (coo) (coo)…**♫

…well, sort of like pigeons walking.

♫**Dancin' a little smidgen of the kind of ballet/ that sweeps me away…**♫

His flat feet made the heel-and-toeing of most dance steps awkward, but…

♫**Doin' the pigeon (coo) (coo)…** ♫

…with the blonde leading the way…

♫**Doin' the pigeon (coo) (coo)…** ♫

…he began to get the hang of…

♫**Doin' the pigeon every day…** ♫

"Oh, there's Bill," said the blonde, leading him toward his returned client. "Let's change partners."

♫**Doin' the pigeon (coo) (coo)…** ♫

The next thing he knew, he was holding the hand of the suspect's tall husband and…

♫**Doin' the pigeon (coo) (coo)…** ♫

…stomping his feet and…

♫**People might smile, but I don't mind…** ♫

…kicking back a foot like a…

♫**They'll never understand the kind of fun I find…** ♫

…like a dancing…

♫**Doin' the…** ♫

Max had a full-blown hunch that *Case of a Runaway Juvenile Delinquent* was in fact only a wild pigeon chase, but…Hmmm? He spotted the kid, standing off to the side, jotting notes in a small spiral notebook, no doubt for that half-awake P.I. up in Okmulgee named Owsley.

WEDNESDAY
April 13, 2022

CHAPTER SIX

After dropping off his mom at the suburban Oklahoma City office building where Dr. Pfau marketed magnetized shoes, Max eyeballed the letter-size brochure handed to him by the dancing blonde at last night's meeting of Fine Feathered Friends.

According to the one-page flyer, World of Wings was a ten-acre attraction located in OKC's so-called Adventure District that also included a zoo, science museum and horse racing track. Noted centerpiece of the attraction was an American Pigeon Museum & Library, advertised by written blurb as *the go-to source for anything and everything you ever wanted to know about man's oldest and best friend.*

He had no old pigeon friends and didn't want to know anything about the birds. He'd taken on *Case of a Runaway Juvenile Delinquent* only because that wiseguy, Owsley—aided and abetted by the kid—was poaching in his stomping grounds. But he had time on his hands, so…Max goosed the brown boiler and headed for the nearby source of unwanted poop.

Pigeons lazing on public benches and crapping on sidewalks were like homeless bums in his book. Instead of earning seeds by, say, singing songs, they lived fat-and-happy off peanuts and popcorn conned from suckers who happened to pass by. And they all looked alike, which made tracking down Homer Crowe like trying to find a particular hair of a bird in a bush.

In other words, no way was he onto a lay such as *Case of The Maltese Falcon* that made Sam Spade famous.

Arrived at the address of the so-called World of Wings, he got out of the boiler and ankled toward a one-story red brick building. A sign identified the joint as *American Pigeon Museum & Library*, but in cages out front…

"Yes, they are all pigeons," said a youngish dame holding a watering can, to describe the collection of odd birds on display. "Distinctly different in appearance, mainly because they were bred by fanciers to emphasize certain traits evolved over thousands of years from the same ancestor, the so-called Rock Dove."

Hmmm. That was useful poop, Max had to admit. Since all pigeons didn't look alike after all, maybe he would circulate a photo of Homer Crowe and get lucky.

A name tag identified the short-haired gal as a Miss Docent, who seemed to work there and in fact seemed to have a pigeon-toed foot condition like his mom. A sign on one cage identified its occupant as "Curly". And in fact the bird's bluish feathers did look like they had been done up in a beauty parlor.

"She's a Frillback, and loves to be held."

Max declined the dame's offer to hold the winged rat. A childhood pet named Tommy Turtle—who never even peeked out of its shell and never moved—was the only live animal he had ever put his mitts on.

"And this is Madonna," she said, pointing at a fowl with feathers bunched up around its neck like the collar of a fancy fox fur coat. "A Jacobin breed, and yes, she is a diva.

"Over here are Jezebel and Don Juan, both Pouters," the Docent dame next said, bobbing her head back and forth as she led him across a sidewalk to some other cages occupied by other odd specimens of so-called fine feathered friends. "Their puffed up crops, which is a term for pigeon gullets, are quite seductive to members of the opposite sex, despite the reputations of pigeons and doves—they're the same thing—for sexual fidelity to a single mate.

"Also beware of Miss Wonderly; she is a Maltese Pigeon…"

Miss Wonderly? Maltese Pigeon? Max's ears perked up.

"… and quite mischievous."

But no, this "Miss Wonderly", with all-white feathers and longish legs, looked like a chicken. Obviously, she was not a feathered version of the *femme fatale* that pulled a fast one on Sam Spade in *Case of The Maltese Falcon* or could have lured Homer Crowe into trouble.

Pigeons were different in personality as well as appearance, according to Miss Docent. They were intelligent enough to recognize themselves in mirrors as well as different people in pictures; and fun to be around, she claimed, bobbing her head toward a cage containing a smallish bundle of black-and-white feathers. "Take Rollo, for instance," she cooed. "He is a Parlor Roller, a favorite of upper-class British fanciers and others who breed them to compete in backward somersault races."

Somersaults? Had Bill Crowe trained Homer to roll head-over-heels from Birmingham, Alabama to Henryetta, Oklahoma, in backward somersaults?!

"No, no, unlike plain tumblers that do backward somersaults in mid air, Parlor Rollers don't take wing. They race across football fields and carpeted rooms. You're thinking of trained homing pigeons that fly in long-distance races back to their respective lofts. Follow me. I'll show and tell all you would ever want to know about mankind's oldest and best friend."

Inside the museum, the gabby Miss Docent explained that all racing pigeons were Homers—dog-gone-it—with an inbred instinct to always return to a loft where they were hatched or otherwise came to cherish at a young age.

At the entrance to a large room, a placard set on a three-legged stand put Max wise to the ins-and-outs of Bill Crowe's hobby:

Pigeon Racing

Pigeon racing is the sport of releasing trained homing pigeons for return to lofts across prescribed minimum distances ranging from 60 to 600 miles. The time it takes birds to reach their home destinations is electronically determined, and the contestant that registers the fastest average speed is declared the winner.

*****

Pigeon races are flown by a specific breed of bird bred for the sport, the Racing Homer. Competitors are trained and conditioned to fly in cross-country races that can be won or lost by seconds. To determine each bird's exact flight time, an identifying band is put on one leg and a computer chip on the other. Each bird is electronically scanned at its release point, and nowadays its arrival home is most commonly registered automatically by loft RFID pads similar to those used at supermarket check-out counters. Winning speeds typically average around 40 to 50 miles per hour, non-stop, depending on prevailing winds and other conditions.

*****

Pigeon racing was introduced to the United States in about 1875. According to the American Racing Pigeon Union, there are currently 15,000 registered racing lofts in the U.S. Although the sport has been banned in Chicago since 2004, racing of Homers remains particularly popular in the New York City areas of Coney Island and Hoboken, New Jersey. Harry Potter's son and heir, Albus, is known to prefer pigeon racing to wizardry.

Contents of the large room consisted of wall-mounted placards listing names of pigeons and pigeon trainers, dates of big races in the past, and other boring info. Shelves were lined with dusty old wood boxes with embedded clocks once used for timing races… beer steins adorned with names and insignia of pigeon racing clubs from mainly Europe… and rusty old trophies.

"And of course there's high stakes betting," said the museum guide. "According to an investigation by PETA — that's 'People for Ethical Treatment of Animals' — a quarter of a million dollars has been wagered on a single race. Which of course leads to cheating. In Japan not long ago, race results were overturned when it was discovered that the owner of one entrant had snagged his racer in flight and boarded it onto a bullet train. Five years ago, the outcome of the Tarles Grand National from France to England was overturned when it was discovered the 'winner' was found to have registered decoys at the starting gate, then 'clocked-in' his racers that had remained in their home loft."

Max unsuccessfully attempted to stifle a yawn, but…

"In addition to the many other services homing pigeons have provided to mankind, they were our first mailmen and mailwomen," Miss Docent announced. "Oh yes, we have glorified the man who ran twenty-six miles from Marathon to Athens with news, but have forgotten the birds who delivered mail faster at greater distances across more dangerous territory. Snow, rain, and gloom of night are nothing compared to hawks, falcons, and human predators who stood between Homers and their appointed tasks.

"If a Homer instead of a fat friar had been on the job, Romeo and Juliet would not have come to their tragic ends, no matter what Dr. Fauci said!

"Oh yes, because of plague, Friar John cowered in quarantine rather than deliver Friar Laurence's message to Romeo that Juliet was only drugged; not in a dead condition that would drive her mournful lover to kill himself," said the young pigeon know-it-all, before pausing her obviously memorized spiel with a big grin.

"Today, top-flight Homers win tens of thousands of dollars for their fanciers in races, and even more as breeders. Just last year a bird named Armando was sold to a Belgian breeder for over a million dollars."

Holy cow! A million smackers was in the ballpark of what that bird statue was thought to be worth when Sam Spade took on *Case of the Maltese Falcon*! No wonder Bill Crowe had hired him to…

"A million dollars is nothing compared to the many other contributions the noble Homers have made to the welfare of mankind," said Miss Docent, bobbing her head almost frantically as she danced toward the doorway to another room. "Follow me."

An olive-drab trailer such as would have been hooked up to a military Jeep was parked in the center of the other large room. Wood boxes with chicken-wire doors were mounted on its rear. One of those dummies used by stores to display clothes stood next to the trailer, displaying a U.S. Army uniform with attached mesh pouch holding a stuffed pigeon.

On a wall, a placard—boldly headlined **Other Pigeon Contributions to Warfare**—said: **Saltpeter used for making gunpowder was produced by**…But another placard that caught Max's eye was headlined **Courageous Military Pigeons.**

Topping a printed list was a bird named Cher Ami, described as a medal-winning hero that saved one hundred and ninety-four human lives by delivering a wartime message tied to its almost severed leg, despite also losing one eye and being shot in the chest by enemy fire. Farther down the list…Yeah, there was G.I. Joe, the hero who had inspired Bill Crowe's old man to inspire Bill to inspire Homer to win a big Dixie Classic race and no doubt lots of money. But…

"Another platoon of pigeons serving in Italy during World War II were not so lucky," said Miss Docent, pointing toward a framed poster for a movie titled *The Pigeon Who Took Rome.* "Of twenty-four brave birds smuggled into the Holy City by American spies—intended for use by Italian resistance personnel to send back information about positions of Nazi occupiers—twenty-three were cooked for dinner by a fat Italian man. Only one survived to fulfill its mission."

Max was shocked. Three and a half fried chickens were the most he had ever downed at a single meal.

"That was nothing compared to what men like you did to members of the Passenger breed," said the pigeon-toed dame, bobbing her pointy nose at him, as though he was the fat Italian guy who ate twenty three pigeons for dinner. "Passenger pigeons were once the most numerous birds in North America. On a single day in 1860, a flock of perhaps <u>billions</u> of Passengers blocked out the sun over Toronto, Canada. Now the breed is extinct."

"I have never been to Rome, Italy or Canada, and have never knowingly eaten a single pigeon of any kind in my entire life."

"Maybe not; but other human fatsos ate them, no doubt two and three at a time; and cleared the forests of their sources of seeds and nuts."

"Except for an occasional pecan pie, I hate seeds and nuts!"

In flight from the World of Wings attraction, and Miss Docent, Max admitted to himself that he had been slightly wrong about pigeons. The birds did not all look alike. They had been pioneers of postal service. The speedy ones who raced home were far from worthless. And pigeons had bravely served in wartime.

In other words, while the bird statue recovered by Sam Spade in *Case of The Maltese Falcon* had turned out to be what the savvy private dick himself admitted was only "the stuff that dreams were made of", Max now realized *Case of a Runaway Juvenile Delinquent* was really *Case of a Misguided Juvenile Hero* that, if solved by him, would be well worth being reported in a podcast *Maximo Morgan Mystery*.

CHAPTER SEVEN

Though showered, dressed, and needing to tend to her birds, Coo lay on her bed; staring at the ceiling as she continued to worry and wonder about what went down at last night's FFF pre-Dixie Classic wingding.

Bert and Bill had acted strangely; there was no doubt about that. During a so-called cocktail hour her usually inattentive husband and her usually slyly attentive illicit suitor had reversed roles. Though bosom buddies since childhood, they had clearly kept their distance from one another. But then they had gone outside together, obviously—to judge by Bert's breath later—to drink something stronger than punch. And Bill was a chronic braggart about his "romantic" escapades, especially when liquored up. Would he have let slip something about her recent flirtation with him?

Equally worrisome, an old postal buddy of Bill's had told her that his prize cock, Homer, had gone missing; and seemed to suggest that she might have something to do with the disappearance of Princess Kasmir's racing rival. Thankfully interrupted by the start of dancing, the fat man had not said more. And neither Bill nor Bert had returned to the party with a bloody nose. Still, she sensed danger in the air.

Finally satisfied that the coast was at least temporarily clear, Coo got up from the bed and went from the bedroom into the kitchen, but…Oh no, Bert was still in the house; standing at the stove, attending to a skillet. He turned to her, sheepishly smirking, and said, "Sorry about Clara Lindsey's hair. But it'll grow back. And, dog-gone-it, Donald was not the one at fault."

Coo maintained the silent treatment she had employed since yesterday morning's incident involving the cut-and-dye customer and her husband's new second-best friend.

After watching and re-watching re-runs of especially idiotic *Saturday Night Live* skits, her equally moronic mate—failing to get the failed attempt at humor—had been inspired by what he took to be the true story of a big-city advertising executive who went into the wild, made friends with a bird of prey named Donald, and became "The Falconer". In particular, he had related to a dumb skit in which Donald supposedly flew to Las Vegas, lived large, and ended up in bed with Alec Baldwin and an old woman who reminded Baldwin of his first grade school teacher.

Like *SNL* writers who must have never heard of Walt Disney, Bert was enthralled with the idea of birds behaving like humans, and/or *vice versa*. Now he himself was a falconer, with his own "Donald".

"You made Clara's hair look like one of your fancy pigeons, and—dog-gone-it—it was Donald's turn to stretch his wings."

Feeling compelled to abandon the silent treatment, Coo ignored Bert's mistaken reference to her trained racers as useless "fancy" pigeons and asked: "What did you and Bill talk about last night while you were boozing outside the VFW Hall?"

"Chicks, as usual" was Bert's answer, said with an especially obscene smirk. "And did you see the move Bill made on Dodo Vogel when the dancin' started? Dodo was one of his girlfriends back in high school, you know."

"Did he say anything about any other high school girlfriend; or anything about his prize cock?"

"Nope, not a word. Dog-gone-it, Coo Coo, I wish you wouldn't go up against Bill's prize cock. I wish the three of us could be friends and hang out together like we did in high school."

Gagging at sight of three runny eggs served by Bert as an obvious peace offering of sorts, Coo bolted from the kitchen and raced toward her lofts.

Two of them were set against a large barn. An upper part of their outward walls were enclosed with wire mesh. Twenty nooks, each large enough for one or pairs of birds lined the back walls of both units. By a side door, she entered the one that housed fifteen breeding hens.

Hoping Homer's lust for Lurleen Lumplin might have overcome his natural instinct to return to his home loft, she first looked…But no, the little vixen assigned to "weaken Homer's wings" roosted all alone in her cubbyhole.

Next, she visually scanned the loft interior for a bird wearing a bright red leg-band such as worn by Bill's racers, but… No, Homer had not been otherwise waylaid, so to speak, on the premises.

After searching the adjacent loft housing her racing hens, Coo looked up to the sky and sighed.

On the one hand, if Homer failed to show up for the Dixie Classic, chances of Princess Kasmir winning at least the Oklahoma bracket of the interstate race would be much improved. On the other hand, if foul play to Bill's cock was suspected, the victory would be marred and she…

With another sigh, Coo recalled that when she was a teenager her figure skating coach—supposedly to teach a lesson about good sportsmanship—had screened an animated *National Lampoon* TV movie titled *Tonya: The Battle of Wounded Knee* that was supposedly based on a true story about a female Olympic skater. She had identified with the Tonya Somebody, whose ex-husband knee-capped her rival. In the end, however, the role model failed to win a medal—supposedly because her panties were too tight during her performance—and afterward became a pariah of sorts.

Hmmm. Coo moved to the side of a small free-standing all-white loft with domed roof, designed and built to roughly resemble the Taj Mahal. Through its glistening silver-mesh front, she looked into the orange eyes of Princess Kasmir.

"Would Bert have sicced Donald on Homer?" she asked aloud. The Princess cooed and bobbed her head, but…No, her hopefully soon-to-be ex-husband would never have risked doing such a thing to his bosom buddy's pride-and-joy, she hoped.

As much or more than the glory and money to be had by winning the Grand Prix of southern pigeon racing, Coo yearned to beat and financially ruin Bill Crowe—a big bettor on races—in revenge for him ruining her life. Not by rejecting her invite to a high school Sadie Hawkins Day dance in favor of Dodo Vogel, at least not exactly. To make the bastard jealous was the foolhardy reason she had seduced his best friend, for which she had paid a terrible price. And all these years later, to gain access to Bill Crowe's prize cock was the reason she had got a boob job, colored her hair blue, and otherwise connived to rekindle the chronic horndog's sexual interest in her by flirting and leading him on with...

OMG! Only now did it dawn on her that a suggestive message attached to Homer's leg...

Coo dropped to the ground in front of the breeders loft and began to frantically search for the small tin cylinder possibly dropped during Homer's launch for home. An enclosed note expressing a false sentiment—if found and misunderstood by Bert—might well provoke "The Falconer" to sic Donald on her!

CHAPTER EIGHT

Max ankled into Mr. Quickie's, sat down at his desk, and fished a tattered old book of *Yellow Pages* from a drawer. During the drive back from Oklahoma City, he had got his mom to turn on her newfangled phone and search for a podcast about private detection. Tuned into a station identified as *True Crime P.I.* run by a dame named Dana Poll…

Aha, into the copy shop came the kid, wearing an old-fashioned felt hat, adult double-breasted suit and floral tie. Obviously, his ex-protege had lost his nerve at last night's FFF dance, and was now crawling back for a second chance to continue working as his case jotter, but…No doubt still embarrassed to face him, the young wannabe private dick veered off toward Quickie's personal workstation.

Listening to the *True Crime P.I.* podcast, he had doped out that *Case of a Missing Tooth* was an almost dead ringer for the one-and-only Brad Runyon lay documented on film: a case titled simply *The Fat Man,* in which a dentist got bumped off by…

Now the kid and Quickie were yukking it up, like old buddies swapping funny jokes. Max continued searching the *Yellow Pages* for a lead on an expert witness for his own planned podcast.

In *The Fat Man* case it turned out that a bad actor rubbed out the dentist and stole his files with intent to do away with evidence of dental work that would have led to identification of another of his victims. In the podcast *Case of a Missing Tooth,* on the other hand, a savvy P.I. grilled two shady dentists and…

Now the kid was ankling toward him, wearing a big toothy grin on his big fat face.

Mom must have punched a wrong button on her phone — or maybe her new magnetized shoes messed with the electronic feed — 'cause it turned out that the two dentists were only debating the pros-and-cons of replacing a patient's missing tooth with either a removable denture or permanent implant. Anyway, now that he had the hang of the new high-tech technique for reporting cases, personal podcasting looked to be a game changer back to the Brad Runyon radio days of *Noir.*

"Dropped by as a professional courtesy," said the kid, before plopping his big butt into a chair and…and…and daring to also plop an oddly shoed foot onto the desk!

"According to my new client, Mrs. Penelope Crowe, your 'runaway juvenile delinquent' named Homer is not her boy. He is her husband's prize racing pigeon. So not to worry, Mr. Maximo; the bird is as good as in hand; probably coming home on its own. Ha, ha, *Your Case of a Runaway Teenager* is as good as closed."

Stunned by the revolting reversal of relationship, Max bit his tongue as the uppity kid went on to tell that Bill Crowe's missus had called "headquarters" after seeing a bench sign advertising that Tom Owsley slept with one eye open. The Okmulgee P.I. had assigned the matter to his new green-as-grass spotter/ jotter and…

"Mrs. Crowe didn't want to hire me at first, not because I looked too young to be a private dick — not in my new outfit — but because I reminded her of you, Mr. Maximo, who she remembered as her husband's ex-co-worker. Even Mr. Quickie says we look like brothers, no doubt because we're both fat, pear-shaped, and almost hairless. But Mr. Owsley got on the blower and set her straight."

Max ground his teeth.

The kid blabbed that Bill Crowe's proverbial better half was a music teacher, who taught young girls to sing in an at-home studio filled with birds. She had told the kid she became suspicious about her husband's extra-curricular activities when he not only did away with his cell phone, but also cut off their land line. And a nosy companion of hers had supposedly confirmed her hunch by repeating overheard poop about "Billing-and-Cooing".

Billing-and-Cooing?

"Hanky-panky, Mr. Maximo. It looks like your postal service buddy has been making time with an old high school girlfriend named Alice Cooper Haggard, who is also legally married."

"So you have sold out to the Owsley snooper," said Max in a tone intended to convey disgust. "Hammer, Spade, Marlowe; all the classy gumshoes back in the *Noir* wanted nothing to do with domestic cases."

"Yeah, that's what they said," the cocky kid replied, "but like you yourself copped to, Mr. Maximo: a private dick has to stay sharp, pay the bills and…Heck, you yourself took on a lay to track down a runaway juvenile delinquent that turned out to be only a pigeon; more like Ace Ventura, pet detective, than Mike Hammer or Sam Spade."

"I doped out the pet detail in a New York minute," Max claimed. "And by the way, wiseguy, in addition to Homer Crowe being worth more than that famous statue that didn't even look like a legit Maltese bird, pigeons have been major players in lots of adventures, especially during wartime."

"You must be referring to *Case of The Telltale Pigeon Feathers*," said the know-it-all bookworm. "But so what?"

Max drew a blank.

"You know. The *Sherlock Holmes Adventure* in which pigeon feathers spotted in the room of a boarding house owned by Mrs. Hudson's sister tipped off Holmes and Watson that a lodger was an enemy spy, using carrier pigeons to send secret messages to the enemy during a Boer War."

Enemy spy! Pigeon messages to Germans! That did it.

"No way, Jose! No way would an All-American pigeon… Have you not heard of G.I. Joe?" Max sputtered. "He's a hero who happens to be stuffed and mounted in New Jersey, for risking his life to save Italian civilians and allied soldiers who were mistaken for Germans!"

"I used to have a G.I. Joe action figure, Mr. Maximo. He was not a pigeon."

"Have you not heard of the twenty-three brave pigeons who got eaten by a fat Italian?" Max ranted. "A single lucky one escaped the pot and saved Rome, Italy from German boars!"

"Nope, never heard of him."

"Pigeons were the first American postal workers, who delivered mail from Italy to Greece through wind, snow, gloom of night and…"

"No personal offense intended, Mr. Maximo. All I meant to say was…Well, since Homer is a homing pigeon and likely on his way back home at this very minute, why don't you join us. Mr. Owsley has all the high-tech equipment for sleuthing, such as… Well, have a gander at these new tracking shoes," said the kid, putting his other oddly shod foot on the desk. "Notice anything special?"

Max scratched his head.

"They're called *Switcheroos*, with heels in the front and toe-shaped soles in back. You case a joint in other footwear, then switch to *Swtcheroos* when you fade the scene. Suspects might see the tracks, but have no clue what's afoot. And *Switcheroos* are comfortable as well as stylish."

Max admitted—silently to himself—that the odd-ball trackers could be a gumshoe game changer.

"C'mon, Big Bro, private dicking together would be like old times. I'll write up our cases and ask Mr. Owsley for permission to send the reports to Mossik Press."

"Beat it, kid," Max barked. "And don't let the swinging door hit your backside on the way out."

It wasn't Bill Crowe's fault he was a born chick magnet. And a hearsay accusation of hanky-panky by his wife's nosy pal, even if true, should not be held against Homer. In addition…

"Maximo Morgan flies solo," he declared, "and in missing pigeon cases always gets the bird."

CHAPTER NINE

At the G&H Decoys Company employee lounge, arrangements for the wedding of Kandi *nee* Something *nee* Keller and Grady Somebody were in place, exactly as Dodo had planned.

Tables and chairs were lined up to signify a bridal path leading from the Men's and Ladies Rooms to the other end of the lounge, where the nuptial knot would be officially tied.

Groom and Justice of the Peace, formally dressed in coats-and-ties and now sobered up for the occasion, had amicably concluded a fuss about fee.

Butch Junior was seated at a folding card table adjacent to a fire exit, manning a boom box that would provide recorded music selected by the bride.

Outside the doorway, a dozen pigeons were bundled into a large overhanging mesh net, from which they would be released by Butch Junior as the newly christened Mr. and Mrs. hurried toward the Fountainblue Motel for their overnight honeymoon.

And now, onlookers began to drift in, along with hopelessly romantic ambience.

Still, as a wedding veteran—both planner and participant—Dodo well knew from experience that the affair was bound to be crashed by the proverbial "Murphy": he who made whatever could go wrong, go wrong, and at the worst possible moment.

A regular feature of the *Tonight Show*, for instance, consisted of countless responses from viewers to an advertised Jimmy Fallon hashtag—*#WeddingFails*— that ran the gamut from accounts of embarrassing wardrobe malfunctions to drunken bridesmaids to tipped over wedding cakes, etcetera, etcetera, etcetera.

At the last minute of her own first nuptial event—the one with Butch Senior—her future father-in-law had blocked invited guests— including Bill Crowe—from entering the church after her future mother-in-law had adamantly demanded that the best man and ushers make immediate cash reimbursements of tuxedo rental deposits before performing their assigned duties. As a result, a feeling of loneliness had come over her as she marched down the aisle to the recorded Toby Keith song of *How Do You Like Me Now?!* At the altar, teary-eyed, she had blurted vows to, not to Butch Senior by name but to Bill.

Fortunately, the still photos, if not the video recording, had turned out well.

And at her second wedding she had inadvertently made the same error. Her groom, Howard Somebody, had not seemed to mind what their marriage counselor later described as only a "Freudian slip". But Billy had been in attendance with his own new spouse, Penelope, who made an ugly scene that somewhat marred the otherwise lovely event.

Thankfully, for her fond remembrance of that special day in her life, the wedding photographer had got a shot of Billy in the foreground of one picture.

Dodo sighed. In hindsight, it was probably those mishaps wrought by "Madman Murphy" that had led her to safely choose another "Bill" for her third walk down the aisle, she now thought. If only that marriage had turned out half as well as the wedding album.

Dodo again sighed. On the bright side, if not for her own experiences with "Murphy" she might not have heard her calling to become a wedding planner. Thanks to her careful arrangements, hopefully, today's bride would have memories of her special day unsullied by anything worse than photobombing by an obnoxious brat or…

At sight of the Justice of the Peace and groom taking their places and looking toward the opposite end of the room, Dodo put her iPhone to her eye and commenced to record the unfolding of another hopelessly romantic event.

🎵**Our little boy is four years old and quite a little man**🎵 played loudly on the boom box, as the bride's little boy from her prior marriage came out of the Men's Room, holding a pillow that, uh oh, should have had rings set on it.

🎵**So we spell out the words we don't want him to understand…**🎵 Though unusual for a wedding, Dodo approved of the bride's hopelessly romantic choice of song famously sung by Tammy Wynette.

🎵**Like t-o-y or maybe s-u-r-p-r-i-s-e…**🎵 Out of the Men's Room, next came the bride's ex.

🎵**Our d-i-v-o-r-c-e becomes final today…**🎵 From the ladies room came the bride.

🎵**I love you both and this will be h-e-double l…**🎵 Arm in arm, down the aisle they marched…a strip of toilet paper serendipitously stuck to a shoe trailing the proud ex-husband like the train of a conventional wedding dress…the bride's face covered not by a conventional veil, but in keeping with her blue denim dress, occupation and budget, a newly whitewashed welder's mask otherwise worn when she painted duck decoys.

🎵**Oh I wish we could stop this d-i-v-o-r-c-e**🎵 At a card table serving as an altar, "Who giveth this woman from matrimony?" said the Justice of Peace.

"I do," said the bride's ex-husband, bowing to place a sheet of paper on the altar.

After picking up the one-page document, putting on reader specs and turning his smiling face to the bride, "Do you, Kandi, accept this official title to a 2010 Chevy van in settlement of any and all claims against this man from this day forward, for richer and poorer, in sickness and in health?"

"I do."

"And you, uh, young man," the officiator said after turning a stern face to the groom, "do you solemnly accept joint responsibility with this woman for all outstanding amounts due or to become due on this pre-owned vehicle until death do you part?"

"I do."

Looking back to his right, "I now pronounce you two divorced," said the "Marrying Sam", before again looking left, "and I hereby pronounce you two to be man-and-wife. You may both kiss the bride."

♫**People may smile, but I don't mind…** ♫

Dodo moved into the aisle and backed toward the exit as she filmed…

♫**They'll never understand the the kind of fun I find…** ♫

…the happy threesome dance toward the door…

♫**Doin' the pigeon (coo) (coo)…** ♫

…to the tune Butch Junior must have picked out.

♫**Doin' the pigeon (coo) (coo)…** ♫

Barely outside, she pointed her iPhone upward and…

♫**Doin' the pigeon (coo) (coo)…** ♫

Oh no, Butch Junior's pigeons, highly agitated and obviously desperate to fly home to his coop, seemed to be tangled in the mesh netting.

♫**People smile, but I don't mind…** ♫

No doubt poop would come raining down and…

♫**They'll never understand the the kind of fun I find…** ♫

Sure enough, "Murphy" had struck with a vengeance, Dodo thought, but…No, the birds broke free and…

Ping!

Beneath the music blaring through the open fire exit, a sound of something metallic hitting the pavement made Dodo think one of her lucky heart-shaped earrings had dropped off.

♫**Doin' the pigeon (coo) (coo)…** ♫

She bent over, visually searched the sidewalk and…

♫**Doin' the pigeon (coo) (coo)…** ♫

…found lying there, not her earring but a small tin cylinder, and…

♫**Doin' the pigeon (coo) (coo)…** ♫

Inside the little container, Dodo discovered a rolled-up piece of paper with handwriting on it.

Hmmm?

CHAPTER TEN

At the wheel of his mom's boiler, Max kept pedal-to-the-metal as he raced down a dirt road about ten miles west of town. Yeah, it was almost supper time, Mom would be wondering why he was not at the kitchen table. But the re-named *Case of A Misguided Juvenile Hero* had turned into a personal slugfest: Maximo Morgan versus The Kid: him wearing two-tone wing-tipped gumshoes and fighting out of Bill Crowe's corner; his opponent wearing *Switcheroos* and trunks of Bill's suspicious wife, so to speak.

The kid's below-the-belt double-cross had caught him off guard. Now, however, he again had his wits about him. And ring-savvy wits beat fancy footwork in nine out of ten knock-down, drag-out heavyweight bouts.

One of the first rules of private dicking was to never believe a client, especially if the client happened to be a dame. In *Case of The Maltese Falcon*, for instance, yeah, Spade accidentally got his partner bumped off by taking on a lay for a "Miss Wonderly", but Miles Archer was a no good louse who knew the score before pocketing more than his fair share of the fee. And as Sam later explained to the *femme fatale*, quote: "We didn't exactly believe your story. We believed your two hundred dollars. You paid us more more than if you had been telling the truth."

While he himself did not yet know if Bill Crowe's better-or-worse half was a *femme fatale*, he knew the suspicious wife had given the kid a bum steer. Though a chick magnet by hair and a playboy by nature, no way would Bill have been involved in hanky-panky with an Alice Cooper Haggard, who had to be the same-named broad his client had fingered at the FFF affair as the prime suspect in the disappearance of Homer!

On the other hand, as he himself had learned the hard way as a wet-behind-the-ears kid, even supposedly innocent babes of tender age would sometimes drop a hanky behind a guy to try to lure him into panky. In other words, the Haggard broad could be setting a honey trap, and Bill's wife might have picked up on the vibe. He would have grilled the suspect last night, but music and pigeon dancing broke out and…

Roadside signs flashed by…Max slammed on the brakes… put the boiler into reverse gear, and backtracked.

A rusting painted sign nailed to a post said:

La Maison Derriere Loft

Breeding & Hair Done by Appointment Only

A newer-looking sign on another post said:

BEWARE OF BIRD!

Max steered the boiler onto a rutted dirt driveway, drove toward a cluster of farm buildings, and parked. On foot, he saw no signs of life, human or animal, on land or in the air. All was eerily quiet except for gusts of wind.

Up on the rickety front porch of a house, he battened down his fedora with a tug and knocked on a sagging screen door. No one answered. "Anybody home?" he hollered. Not a peep in return. Determined to get in the Haggard broad's face, Max ankled around a side of the house and…

Coo. Coo. Coo…

…heard someone calling to the suspect.

Coo. Coo. Coo…

With ears perked up, he ankled toward two sheds set against the backside of a barn.

Coo. Coo. Coo…

They were pigeon coops, to judge by the chicken-wired windows and the louder sounds of…

Coo. Coo. Coo…

… and, hello, he heard someone saying, "Be patient, my dear. Only two more days 'til the Grand Prix, and we will be free at last."

Max sidled up to a third, smaller free-standing coop that looked sort of like a castle version of an over-size dollhouse.

"Lurleen did her job," said someone in a hushed woman's voice. "Miss Lumpkin 'weakened the poor sap's wings' and then some."

Coo. Coo. Coo…

"In fact, the nyphomaniacal little tramp may have overdone the hanky-panky."

Coo. Coo. Coo…

"I've not wanted to upset you with the news but, well, Homer didn't make it home, and, uh, it looks like he may have been, uh, knee-capped."

Coo. Coo. Coo…

"You must not get your panties in a bunch, so to speak. You must stay strong and race as though our lives depend on you winning, which may in fact be the case."

Coo. Coo. Coo…

"We may have to flee before nosy people begin asking questions and jumping to…"

Max lurched in front of the little coop, looked through a wire mesh window and said, "Gotcha!"

The bluish-haired, self-incriminated suspect bolted out a side door of the dollhouse and got in his face. "You again!" she said, with a look of surprise in her black eyes. "Did Bill send you? Did his prize cock make it home with my…?"

"Yeah, Bill put me onto you, Sister. Maximo Morgan's the name, private dicking is my game. Did you have 'Lurleen' knee-cap your competition in the big race, or did you yourself…?"

"Don't be ridiculous. As I told you last night at the FFF meeting, I have done nothing with Homer Crowe except rid him of lice and send him home."

"Don't try to pull the rug over my private eye, Sweetheart. I just now overheard you cop to foul play. Whoever is hiding in that coop might as well come out now, before I throw my weight around."

"You're making a big mistake," said the broad, fluffing her hair as she looked left and right, up and down. "I was talking to my prize racing hen, Princess Kasmir."

Max again peered into the coop and…

Coo. Coo. Coo…

…detected only a pigeon, perched on a post and pooping.

"The Princess likes to watch TV, but I don't bring her into the house on nights leading up to races. She's a big fan of…I was reminiscing with her about her favorite episode of *The Simpsons*, the one titled 'Homer's Night Out' in which Homer Simpson becomes enthralled with an exotic fan dancer, coincidentally named Princess Kasmir."

Hmmm. Max himself was a *Simpsons* fan. He vividly recalled the time Marge threw a fit about Homer attending a so-called bachelor party at a joint called the Sapphire Lounge, where he got photographed dancing onstage with a typical *femme fatale*. In other words, the suspect's story added up, but…

"Let's have a gander inside those other coops."

If Homer Crowe was a playboy like his namesake, chances were he would have returned to *Maison Derriere* after getting de-liced.

"You are trespassing, Mr. Morgan, and Donald is out and about," said the lofts proprietor, no doubt referring to the tall husband who had been with her last night at the VFW. "Donald doesn't take kindly to strangers, so for your own safety, I strongly suggest that you leave without delay."

Max ignored the dodge and ankled over to the other coops. The suspect followed. Obviously nervous as a proverbial pigeon among proverbial cats, she again looked up into the sky, then down to the ground, and…

Coo. Coo. Coo…

"Someone has been nosing around my lofts."

Coo. Coo. Coo…

Max detected no signs of entry, but…Sure as ten dimes made a dollar, shoe prints had been left in soft dirt by someone who had recently faded from a coop by way of a side door.

Coo. Coo. Coo…

"OMG! Donald has been afoot! And…And…From afar, I never realized how big he's become!"

Coo. Coo. Coo…

Max detected other tracks that looked like those of a…

Coo! Coo! Coo!…

Something suddenly blocked the sunlight… Max sensed an overhead swooping movement…Ouch!…The shadow passed… He looked up and…Into the sky went his fedora—possibly along with a piece of his ear—carried not by wind but by some kind of thieving fowl!

THURSDAY
April 14, 2022

CHAPTER ELEVEN

At the kitchen table after breakfast, Max continued to review case notes he had jotted in a small spiral notebook following yesterday's grilling of Alice Cooper Haggard:

4/13/22, 4:52 p.m.—Received medical treatment by suspect, during which she copped to attaching a written message for Bill Crowe to Homer Crowe's leg before releasing the prize cock. Just "pigeon talk", she said, but possibly misunderstood by anyone (such as her husband) who read it "out of context". Mrs. Hag repeatedly cursed Donald Haggard; suggested he may have intercepted Homer and "eaten him for spite".

4/13/22, 5:21 p.m.—Being driven home by the ex-suspect, also in tears, copped to working the lay for Bill Crowe based on suspicion that she had waylaid his racing pigeon. She understood just doing my job; said it was savvy to suspect a Dixie Classic rival would have had a hand in "knee-capping" Homer.

Clarified that opening of case and grilling her was based on <u>client's</u> unfounded suspicion.

Copped also to having inside info that…

OK, he had played the stool pigeon, but for worthy cause.

Dished to victim of idle gossip that client's wife hired rookie P.I. to investigate no doubt also unfounded suspicion of husband's hanky-panky with her. Victim cursed client's wife; suggested the suspicious missus might have intercepted Homer's return home and misinterpreted the attached message before knee-capping the bird.

4/13/22, 5:40 p.m.—Arrived home. Introduced innocent victim to Mom, who insisted the angel of mercy stay for warmed-up supper. Pot roast and mashed potatoes with extra gravy. Hot buttered dinner rolls. Pecan pie and ice cream. Seconds, and thirds. Mom compared angel of mercy to famous Florida nightingale and sympathetically agreed with victim that anyone who used a "widowhood racing technique" deserved any foul play his bird may have run into. Hoped Coo's pigeon would win the Dixie Classic

3/13/22, 8:30 p.m. — Mom drove new best friend home in boiler. Yours truly jotted notes; went to bed with aching ear.

"Max!"

Max turned his head. Through the unbandaged ear he heard his mom say that Doctor Sawyer would be busy all day, playing golf, and that he should soak his head and go back to bed.

No way, Jose´. In addition to hopefully rescuing Homer Crowe, no way would Maximo Morgan stand by and allow the no-account kid to ruin the reputation of an innocent nightingale.

"Max! Mrs. Haggard—I repeat, **Mrs.** Haggard—is a married woman. Do not got back out there to look for that missing pigeon. Don't get caught in the switches between the poor girl and that abusive husband of hers."

Yeah, Coo was hitched, but also yeah, to a no-account husband. Driving into town late yesterday, the angel of mercy had also confided to him that "Donald" hovered over her like a dark cloud, and was a constant threat to Princess Kasmir. She had openly wondered if, in fact, her husband and his best friend—Bill Crowe—might be in cahoots with other so-called "Reverends" to "fix" the Dixie Classic. In other words, maybe a plot to knee-cap the Princess had backfired on them, and Homer got caught in the switches.

"Or it could be that Homer came down with, uh, 'weakened wings','"she said, "in which case Bill may have lethally 'scratched' his bird to get out of an unaffordable betting loss."

"Max!" his mom shouted. **"Go soak your head! Those are doctor's orders!"**

No way were a doctor's no-go orders going to fly; not with Maximo Morgan, a veteran mailman following in the footsteps of G.I. Joe. A fellow carrier was missing in action, possibly a victim of foul play. And now—while that turn-coat kid chased his own tail in an unfounded domestic case—he himself had a load of "registered mail" to deliver, so to speak, to multiple new suspects.

Max took pencil in hand and jotted: *Coo Haggard's jealous husband, Donald Haggard…Client's jealously suspicious wife, Penelope Crowe…And even his old postal service buddy and client himself…Bill Crowe.*

Yeah, all three were suspects in the disappearance of Homer Crowe. Any of them could prove to be guilty of "fowl play" of the kind called most foul. *Case of A Misguided Juvenile Hero* could turn out to be a case of murrrderrr; perfect for today's first podcast of a *Maximo Morgan Mystery*.

CHAPTER TWELVE

♫*Stop all trains, and close all roads/ There's a mystery up Harlem way...*♫

With an old song running through her head—a song often sung to her by her father during her early childhood—Coo drove her pickup toward town. She was traveling the route Homer would have taken on a homeward flight from hers to Bill Crowe's loft, but...

♫*Now, who stole the bird? Won't you bring him back/ That bird could really swing...*♫

Unless Bill was playing some kind of pre-race mind game, something had happened to intercept the prize cock on its way.

♫*Coo Coo, Coo Coo/ My coo coo bird could swing...*♫

Power lines often felled pigeons, she hopefully noted as she passed under a stretch of high wires.

♫*At six o'clock, he'd come on the hour/ And here's the way he'd sing...*♫

One or more natural pigeon predators—not necessarily Donald—might have done in Homer.

♫*Coo Coo, Coo Coo/ That's how that bird would sing...*♫

Again it occurred to Coo that her assigned "lovebird", Lurleen Lumpkin, may have overly weakened Homer's wings, leaving him with not enough stamina for even a ten mile sprint.

♫*Coo Coo, Coo Coo/ My coo coo bird could swing...*♫

Whatever the cause of the racing cock's possibly dead status, the little tin cylinder attached to his leg could now be lying harmlessly in some remote field, she told herself as she passed by an abandoned graveyard on the edge of town.

🎵*Coo Coo, Coo Coo...* 🎵

Even better, her indiscreet written message to Bill might now be safely lodged in the intestinal tract of a raccoon, she hoped as she drove onward.

🎵*Coo Coo, Coo Coo...* 🎵

But she could not count on such luck, Coo reminded herself as she arrived at the local post office.

🎵*Stop all trains, close all roads/ There's a mystery up Harlem way...* 🎵

Almost thirty minutes later, still waiting in line, Coo seethed as Bill Crowe leaned closer to a broad-beamed female postal customer at the counter and continued to aggressively flirt. The Don Juan act had become tiresome even from afar, she was thinking when… It hit her like a pie in the face: Bill's constant over-the-top clownish attempts at womanizing was in fact an "act".

She had often thought of Bert's psychotic loathing of pigeons as somehow rooted in peer group reaction to his performance in a long ago junior high school theatrical skit. Previously known only as Gary Lee Haggard, his black unibrow, mirthless hacking laugh and all-around dorkiness had made him the perfect choice to play "Bert" in a production of *Sesame Street Christmas*. And predictably, following the first of three performances inside the school auditorium her unlikely future mate had been mercilessly mocked by other students for his robust off-key rendition of a song about how much he <u>loved</u> pigeons.

"Any chance of getting a little man-to-man service around here?" a man in line ahead of her shouted.

Following a second performance, again showing Bert in a bathtub, finding Ernie's beloved rubber ducky underwater, and deciding to sell his own beloved paper clip collection in order to buy a soap dish for his bosom buddy's toy, "Hey, Billy, don't bend over to pick up the soap!" someone in the audience had yelled when Bill Crow came onstage in the role of Ernie.

"Hey, buddy, get a room!" the man impatiently waiting for postal service now shouted at Bill.

By time the curtain rose for the *Sesame Street* skit's third and final performance, not only fellow newly teenaged members of the junior high school student body had begun to openly snicker that "Bert" and Bill were gay. When Bill went to a drugstore to sell his rubber ducky in order to buy Bert a cigar box for his bosom buddy's beloved collection of paper clips, "Hey, Billy," the school's basketball coach had yelled, "get a Monica 'cigar box' for yourself! You might like it!"

And since then, just as Gary Lee—stuck for life with the "Bert" moniker—had displayed mentally unbalanced hatred of pigeons...

"Damnit, you don't have to lick the stamps for her!"

...it was now clear to Coo that Bill Crowe's relentlessly offensive show of being an insatiable heterosexual "cocksman" was a defensive reaction of sorts.

After another postal clerk came on duty and other would-be postal customers formed a new que, Coo moved to next in Bill's line. To the departing customer in front of her, he said, "Sorry, most women like a man's sticky tongue."

She herself then leaned over the counter.

"Whoa," said the Romeo, looking left, then right. "For crying out loud, Coo, not here; not in a public post office!"

"I'm here to report lost, possibly stolen 'mail'. Not to get my already sticky stamps licked."

"Lotsa luck with that. There are forms over at that table you can fill out, but I wouldn't hold my breath."

"The correspondence was confidential, intended for you and...Is it true Homer has gone missing, or is his 'disappearance' some kind of pre-Grand Prix pretense? Did you knee-cap your weakened cock to get out of a losing bet?"

"How do you happen to know Homer is...not home?"

"That fat private detective—the useful idiot you hired to cover your ass—told me I was your prime 'suspect' for Homer's 'misguided juvenile heroism'."

"Damnit, Morgan was way out of line to suspect you. Golly, Coo," the amorous clerk continued in a hushed voice, "you know how I feel about us, and how I feel about my prize cock. If Homer shows up and wins the Dixie Classic prize money, I plan to tell Penelope that we…<u>Are</u> you my prime suspect? Did you waylay Homer to give Princess Kasmir an unfair advantage?"

"I released Homer days ago, with a message to you attached to his leg."

"Oh yeah? What was the message?"

"Let's just say it was somewhat akin to the sappy notes you have been attaching to Princess Kasmir before sending her back to me."

"Aha! I knew you would give in. I knew you still had the hots for me."

"Uh hum, and probably Penelope would also see things that way—and *vice versa*—if the message happened to fall into her hands."

"Are you threatening me, Coo? Are you trying to make me scratch my prize cock two days before the Dixie Classic? Well, it won't work. Penelope knows she married a chick magnet. She clucks like a wet hen, but would never actually…"

"Your wife has already 'actually' hired her own private detective, who may have nabbed Homer…"

"What a little sneak!"

"…and may have taken possession of my message."

"That's a federal offense!"

"Or Donald may have snatched Homer in mid-flight, and delivered the goods to Bert."

"Big Bert?! Oh my God. Coo, what are we going to do?"

Coo put a small tin cylinder on the counter. The capsule contained another note, she explained. In her unmistakable handwriting, she had expressed her true feelings about…

Bill shrank from the shiny little object as though it were loaded with explosives.

The note made clear how much she despised him, Coo continued. And confessed in brief that she had engaged in co-training exercises with his prize cock only to "weaken Homer's wings'" for the Grand Prix.

"What a dirty trick!"

To throw off Penelope-- and possibly Bert—she instructed Don Juan to make sure his suspicious wife and/ or her private detective found the note, hopefully leading them to conclude that it had fallen off his missing cock's leg and…

"Ah, I see; but…Penelope would never fall for the trick. She knows I'm a chick magnet."

"The note ends with a word-for-word repetition of what my note sent with Homer said," Coo further explained. "Hopefully, anyone who reads both messages will think the, uh, friendly words are just my regular sign-off."

"What regular sign-off? Damnit, Coo, what did the note carried by Homer say?"

"Nothing too endearing, or incriminating. Just, 'Coochie Coochie Coo. Guess who?'"

"Got it!" said Bill, grabbing the cylinder. "Sometimes lost mail does accidentally show up."

It was a long shot, Coo conceded to herself as she walked away, but if the private detective working for Penelope Crowe was as clueless as the hopeless moron hired by Bill, the trick might just work.

♫ *We stole the bird from the coo coo clock/ And 'ol Cab Calloway put it in hoc/ Coo Coo, Coo Coo…* ♫

CHAPTER THIRTEEN

Max ankled along Trudgeon Street, turned a corner onto 5th and, uh oh, spotted a stakeout across from the the post office. Instantly, his gumshoe know-how kicked in.

First, to give himself time to think, he stopped in his tracks and looked down at his shoes as though checking to see if he had stepped on, say, a wad of carelessly discarded chewing gum.

Second, he looked up into the air, as if actually thinking.

Third, he patted the chest pockets of his suit jacket and — as though realizing he had left something at his Mr. Quickie workstation — casually doubled back around the corner.

Out of the stakeout's line of sight, he hotfooted toward the rear entrance to his former workplace.

The post office door signed *Employees Only* wasn't even locked. Inside, he found that a large storage area was not even manned. Security at his old stomping grounds seemed to have gotten lax since his last rear entry, Max was thinking, but…No, an unsigned interior door was shut tight.

He tried a secret old entry code embedded in his memory: Knock…Knock Knock Knock…Knock Knock….Bingo.

To the guy who opened the door, he flashed a one-finger salute near the bill of his vintage USPS cap — recalled into service due to yesterday's loss of his fedora — and ankled into the employee lounge known as the Rubber Room.

Postal employees worked under a lot of stress. Anxiety ran high in their hearts and minds. Feet problems were chronic. Heck, the term "go postal" originated at a post office in Edmond, Oklahoma back in the Eighties, after a part-time carrier blew his stack and sparked a national outbreak of USPS workplace violence. Plenty of R&R was essential to calming postal personnel nerves. Regular breaks were mandatory. Currently, for instance, five or six guys were seated at a table, blowing off steam by playing cards.

"Bill Crowe on duty today?" he asked. "Need to have a word with him about a confidential matter."

"Bill's fighting off customers out front," said one of the guys. "Hey, Maxie, what happened to your ear, rough day talking on your private dick 'blower' about 'confidential matters'? Ha, ha, ha…"

"Your head looks swelled up bigger than ever, Max," said another guy. "What the hell, your cap looks like an upside-down teacup setting on a watermelon. Ha, ha, ha…"

"Had a run-in with a birrrd of prey," he explained."Which reminds me," he said after sitting down at the table and now taking a sheet of paper from a pocket. of his jacket."Got a petition here, proposing that our mascot be changed from baldheaded eagle to pigeon."

"Pigeon! You gotta be shitting me, literally. Ha, ha, ha…"

"Yeah, pigeons are good for nothin' but crappin'."

"No way I wear a pigeon patch on my uniform."

Max barely got into telling about G.I. Joe's heroics when…

"Pigeons aren't real," said someone in a high-pitched voice.

Max swiveled his head and…Holy cow! A yardbird named Nelson Strauser was sitting in a darkened corner of the Rubber Room, still in uniform!

Strauser was not one of the regular guys. He had always been a loner, who lived with his mother and, to hear him tell it, used to stay up all night doing experiments on captured songbirds. Caught on camera peeking under a Ladies Room stall — claimed the regular guys were listening to him in the Men's Room — he had been severely reprimanded for hygiene violations and demoted to sorting room assistant, but failed to straighten up and fly right. Facing dismissal, he had blamed his chronic mis-sorting of mail on a nervous tic caused by unrelenting stress; and threatened to sue the United States Postal Service if not put on full-time Rubber Room duty.

All the regular guys laughed in his face, but…As Strauser came out of the shadows, the regular guys in attendance threw in their cards and pushed back their chairs. One-by-one, each said he was rested-and-ready to return to front line flak. Good to see high troop morale, but…As Strauser sat down and put a metal lunch pail on the table, Max recalled hearing that the malcontent's disciplinary board hearing had been abruptly adjourned when he showed up with a thermos suspected of being a disguised bomb. That was years ago, and yet…

"Ever wonder why you have never seen a baby pigeon?" said Stauser, peering at him through green-tinted specs thick as coke-bottle bottoms. "No pigeons have hatched since right after World War II; that's why. Those 'feathered' creatures you see perched on power lines are mechanical drones, recharging batteries to operate their wings and the cameras embedded in their heads. Their so-called poop is highly magnetic!"

The government had started eradicating real pigeons and replacing them with mechanical spies during a Cold War, the oddball claimed.

"Why do you think people stopped eating pigeons?" Strauser asked. "Because a kid in Terre Haute, Indiana died of lockjaw after his dental braces locked onto a highly magnetized pigeon his grandma baked; that's why."

Max had heard of tom turkeys peeping on people, but… "If you don't believe me, check it out at # *pigeonsaren'treal*," said Strauser, with a twitch of his head that scattered dandruff from his mop of greasy dark hair onto his shoulders. "Check it out on TikTok or…"

Tick Tock? Max eyed Stauser's lunch box with ears perked up.

"I know why right-wing nuts like you are so protective of George Washington and Robert E. Lee statues!"

Max visually searched for a Rubber Room fire alarm box, but…

"Hey! Strauser!" said a voice. "No bellowing your loony B.S. in the Rubber Room! Get back in your hole for R&R."

"Back off, Crowe," the irregular guy shouted before picking up his lunch pail and backing himself into the darkened corner. "Your buddy came in here with a petition to make a pigeon our mascot! He's a radical right-wing Reverend just like you!"

Max got up from the table, put the petition back into his jacket pocket, and waved a crooked finger at Bill Crowe. He started to say, "Let's take it outside," but…Just in case there was something to Strauser's conspiracy theory, he sat back down.

"What the hell, Max," said his client, after joining him at the table, "Coo was just now at the counter. Thanks to your loose lips, she knows I put you on her scent to track down Homer."

"Mrs. Haggard is odorless as a Florida nightingale. But she's worried that a message attached to Homer's leg may…"

"That's between me and her, Morgan. Butt out."

"Don'y worry, Bill. Yours Truly has played a few innocent rounds of 'Postman's Knock' in my day. But word to the wise: your spouse has hired a P.I. to investigate hearsay gossip of hanky…"

"I already know all that. I have a plan to deal with Penelope. For crying out loud, Max, do <u>not</u> butt in and screw things up."

"Okay, I just now spotted new evidence to put certain, uh, suspicions to rest, but I gotta ask: What do you yourself know about what happened to Homer?"

"I know nothing. That's why I hired you, old pal."

"Okay, old pal; you're clean in my book, but another word to the wise," Max said at an especially confidential level of voice. "On my way in, I spotted Donald Haggard staked out across the street, watching the comings-and-goings in and out of the post office like a hawk."

"Donald?! In town?! Oh my God! He must have followed Coo, which means…"

"Yeah, looks like the mistakenly jealous husband has his beak in the wind, so to speak.'

His old pal, twitching like a Mexican jumping bean, got up from the table, lurched to a locker, put on what looked to be an old World War II German helmet, and slunked from the Rubber Room.

Max took his spiral notebook from a jacket pocket, picked up a pencil for keeping card game scores from the table, and exed *Bill Crowe* off his list of suspects.

This was not his first rodeo, literally. A couple of years ago, he got wind that a love 'em-and-leave 'em clown passing through town — literally a rodeo clown — had his way with a local doll. Turned out instead that the virgin had been willingly impregnated by an anonymous sperm donor. But before doping out that detail — at the annual Living Legends Rodeo, intending to make the yardbird do right by the victim — he had gone off half-cocked, literally, and shot himself in the foot, literally.

Moral of the story: The word A-S-S-U-M-E sometimes made an ASS out of U until things got set straight by ME.

CHAPTER FOURTEEN

Sitting on a love seat inside her cozy den, Dodo read yet again the note dropped from one of Butch Junior's pigeons at yesterday's somewhat "Murphied" wedding release. As a hopeless romantic and wedding planner often called upon to counsel young would-be brides and grooms, ordinarily she would not have been hesitant to deliver her various mottos, one of which was: "A Justice of the Peace delayed is justice denied." But under current circumstances…

Dodo put the note back into its small tin capsule and sighed. Last year's petition to the local school board had not called for <u>total</u> elimination of so-called SexEd classes. Public demonstrations had not demanded censorship of the <u>entire</u> instructional film—*Fuzzy Bunny's Guide to You Know What*—previously featured in a *Simpsons* family TV episode. In court afterward, she had explained to a judge that her hurling of a so-called "Molotov Cocktail" had been in objection to only the "Honeymoon" segment of the film, and the hopelessly unromantic claim that new brides often "fake it", but…

There she now sat, single parent of an uneducated seventeen-year-old boy who was in dire need of receiving "The Talk".

With another sigh, Dodo got up from the love seat, put the tin capsule in a purse, picked up a canvas tote, and headed for her son's backyard pigeon loft.

Butch Junior was too young for a serious female relationship, which was one of the reasons she had banned all social internet use and encouraged his interest in pigeons. Now it looked like her plan had backfired. The come-hither note—*Coochie Coochie*

Coo. Guess who?—had obviously been sent by a girl who shared the bird hobby. The conniving little vixen was likely also a junior in high school, and a typical teenaged "Henryetta Hen" scheming to snare Butch Junior in marriage before he graduated and went off to college.

After finding her endangered son inside his loft, Dodo ignored a few pigeon droppings, sat down on a stool and got right to the point.

"Butch Junior, when a boy and a girl think they love each other very much…"

"Aw, Mom, is this gonna be about bees spreading pollen and birds hatching eggs?"

"No, nothing about wildlife," she answered, taking two dolls from her tote and putting them on her lap: her old Bridal Barbie facing upward, and her son's old G.I. Joe on top.

"Aw, Mom…"

To be absolutely clear, she next took a standard electrical extension cord from the tote; one end equipped with a plug, the other with a socket.

"Aw, Mom…"

"I just want to show you what this 'coochie coochie cooing' can lead to," she said, taking the tin capsule containing the note from her purse and…

"Where did you get that?" said Butch Junior, obviously pretending to be only slightly interested. Dodo explained that she had not been snooping; that the evidence of what he had been up to had literally fallen into her lap, not just then but during yesterday's wedding release.

Butch Junior admitted that the capsule must have been attached to a leg of a "captive bird".

Captive bird?

To her bewildered maternal dismay, her son announced he was a "dooman". But to her maternal relief went on to explain that he had acquired a Horseman Pouter named Homewrecker that competed against other pigeons of that breed in contests to capture as many birds as possible during a given time span.

Horseman Pouters, female and male, mainly targeted wild pigeons, said Butch Junior, but sometimes would win extra points by luring and capturing prize birds from racing lofts.

That sounded like innocent shenanigans, but... "Seduction" was Homewrecker's main means of capture, her seventeen-year-old son mumbled.

Oh dear.

"Homewrecker has stayed close to home for the past few days, but might have re-bedded a previously captured pigeon that had got, uh, 'comfortable' in my loft and came back here after getting untangled at yesterday's wedding release. If I still have the bird I'll get extra points in this week's contest against Chip Crowe," said Butch Junior, fiddling with the tin capsule.

"Chip Crowe? Bill Crowe's chip off his block?"

"Yeah, I think that's his old man's name. But Mom, please don't tell Mr. Crowe that me and Chip have been flighting around his loft. Yeah, 'horseman' is a Scottish word for 'highwayman' or 'robber'—people over there bred and trained their Pouters to capture other pigeons for the dinner table—but dooing is now just a sport. We don't eat the captives. If Homewrecker lured a..."

"Show me Mr. Crowe's cock!"

"Aw, Mom, dooing is not really thieving. We set them free every Sunday morning after adding up scores."

Dodo visually scanned a wall of nooks, almost all occupied by look-alike pigeons, but...

"Yep, this little horndog is wearing a red band alright," said Butch Junior, taking a pigeon in hand. "His name is 1632," said her clever son—and after further inspecting the red band on the bird's leg—"sure enough, he's registered as flying for TCN, which is code for 'The Crowe's Nest' racing loft."

"Butch Junior, what have you done?!"

"Sorry, Mom, Homewrecker just does what she's bred and trained to do."

Eying Bill Crowe's feathered protege, Dodo was puzzled. Mister 1632 was bred and trained to fly only homeward after no doubt breaking some female pigeon's heart, which meant…It made no sense that Bill would have attached the suggestive note to his own cock and sent it to himself, but…

It hit her like a hopelessly romantic slap in the face: Bill would have known that Butch Junior was capturing local pigeons in competition with his own boy and…

Dodo snatched the little capsule from the hand of her son. As no less than a hopelessly romantic Academy Award winning actor had recently declared on national TV, love made men do crazy things.

In other words, yes, cockamamie as the scheme might seem to a hopelessly unromantic sort, Bill Crowe, the love of her life, had intended for <u>her</u> to receive the hopelessly romantic come-hither note entrusted to his homer.

CHAPTER FIFTEEN

Max propped up his mom's cell phone, touched one of the electronic gadget's so-called icons, leaned back in his workstation chair and listened. First came the recorded *clomp, clomp, clomping* sounds of Mom's footsteps…next, her recorded voice saying, *There he goes, into that drugstore. He's stepping onto scales…*followed by a throat-clearing sound effect approximating the *cachung* of an old-fashioned ticket dispenser…*Weight: two hundred and forty-six pounds. Fortune: dangerrr. Whooo is it?*

♫Dum dum-dum dum! ♫ his mom semi-sang.

The Fat Mannnn, said his own recorded voice.

To continue the podcast in so-called real time, Max leaned forward, touched another icon and spoke into the phone: "Max Morgan's the name. Private dicking's my game."

♫Dum dum-dum dum! ♫ he semi-sang.

"I was at my desk, boning up on details of Sam Spade's *Case of The Maltese Falcon*, when an old postal service buddy ankled in—lets call him 'Mr. Wonderly'—and reported that his prize racing pigeon, Homer Crowe, had gone missing under mysterious circumstances. That was two days ago.

"Since then, I've doped out multiple theories of the case, fingered and unfingered multiple suspicious characters who may have been involved in the valuable bird's disappearance. Eventually the remaining suspect will crack under my thumb like a rotten walnut, but by then it might be too late. A Grand Prix race is scheduled for tomorrow and the stakes are high.

"What could have happened to Homer Crowe?"

♫Dum dum-dum dum, dum! ♫

Max scooted his chair closer to one occupied by a heavyset guy wearing a hoodless orange hazmat outfit emblazoned U.S. WILDLIFE BUREAU. He adjusted the angle of the cell phone.

"To lend a hand with my investigation, Ranger Ken Mortimer, a pigeon expert officially listed in the *Yellowpages*, is with me today," he announced. "Tell me, Ranger Mortimer, putting aside for the moment the confidential details, suspects and theory of my case, where would a guy look for Homer?"

"Ha! That's a no-brainer. Racers are <u>homing</u> pigeons, duh, naturally equipped with a magnetic compass embedded in their beaks—a tidbit of iron ore called 'magnetite' that interacts with the Earth's magnetic field—and also…"

Max jotted a note to give Homer's home base a once-over, looked up and… noticed the kid come into the copy shop, carrying a large cardboard box.

Hmmm?

"…but that's just navigation. What motivates the male homer to return to its nest at all costs is a strong mating instinct. Especially when his trainer is using the so-called 'widowhood technique', a racing pigeon will fly non-stop for hundreds of miles to get laid."

Max returned his attention to Ranger Mortimer. "Speaking of magnetic fields, if I got someone—say, my mom—to walk around in stylish-but-comfortable *Magno Mocs*, would that magnetically attract Homer to her?"

"Well, pigeons usually mate for life with the same bird, but a puffed up female Horseman Pouter will sometimes divert a male homer from his homeward course. Radical right-wing religious rumor has it that the Holy Ghost visited the Virgin Mary as a pigeon."

Hmmm. Max jotted another note.

"Some errant homers join feral flocks. Some, let's say, simply 'disappear'. Last year in England thousands of racers…"

"Just out of curiosity," said Max, as the kid ankled past him toward the deluxe workstation located farther down a row of cubicles, "what's your expert take on why no one ever sees baby pigeons walking around?"

"Ha! By the look of you, Morgan, I'd say you've likely 'seen' more than your fair share of baby pigeons, taken from their nests within a single month after hatching and served in fancy restaurants as delicacies called 'squab'. Otherwise, pigeons do not leave their nests until full grown at seven or eight weeks of age, so we don't see them 'walking around' as squab."

Max again jotted.

"It used to be that full-grown pigeons were a major food source for everyone," the pigeon expert continued, as the kid ankled back toward the Mr. Quickie exit, without the cardboard box in hand. "Extinction of the so-called Passenger breed was largely due to the many roasted birds and pigeon potpies consumed during the 1800s. Now we depend on peregrine falcons to help take up the slack. Hungry falcons see racing loft landing pads as fast-food service windows. But pigeons are cagy and sometimes get cold feet, even after widowhood training."

Aha, maybe Homer Crowe was just circling Bill's coop to be sure the coast was clear, Max was thinking when…What in Sam Hill? In the kid came again, carrying a second large cardboard box.

"…and of course many racers simply collapse from fatigue," Mortimer was saying, which, aha, raised another possibility that Homer would be found and identified by his lost-and-found leg band.

"Ha!" the wildlife ranger again snorted. "Those racing loft tags are for clocking-in race finishers, not for finding birds that fall by the wayside. Losers, if found, get their necks wrung. Breeders and trainers routinely cull weaklings from their flocks, but…"

The burly expert sighed. "Once upon a time, organized pigeon shoots were popular sport. Hell, shooting captured pigeons was an official event in the 1900 Olympics. Nowadays, Pennsylvania is the only state that still allows large scale pigeon slaughter for fun."

That was a relief, assuming Homer Crowe had not flown to, say, Pittsburgh.

"Yeah, trainers typically do away with eleven out of twelve new birds right off the bat. Sixty percent of those who make the initial cut fail to survive training, during which they are fed once a day and exposed to predators, hunters, power lines and, let's say, 'other dangers' for which they have inadequate survival skills.

"And races expose hardy ones to comparable losses. Just last year in England ten thousand homers that answered the bell and headed for home 'disappeared' during a single day of races. Yeah, a drop in the bucket; and right-wing wing-nuts here in the U.S. of A. are a stubborn bunch. Hell, a typical mating pair of birds breeds six times a year and produces two eggs per clutch. Do the math. It's their high metabolism that makes them do it, and also makes them crap so much from the same vent."

As Ranger Mortimer went on with what sounded like a different tune than what he had expected, Max was again distracted; this time by a guy pushing a dolly past his desk, loaded with what looked to be a large filing cabinet.

"...not enough buckshot in Okmulgee County to make a dent," Mortimer was saying. "Here in town the problem is critical, but not even shotguns and concussion grenades are allowed, much less bazookas. Hell, at the public library highly acidic pigeon poop has about done in that heroic statue of the Doughboy who survived World War I. Droppings have killed all the downtown vegetation, and eaten through the paint of the Mayor's car. In a last ditch effort to save city hall, we have just finished coating all window ledges, railings and other exterior horizontal surfaces with sticky chemical repellents that..."

Aha, Homer Crowe might be stuck on a city hall ledge, Max was thinking when...What the heck, another file cabinet rolled by.

"Pigeon droppings contain saltpeter that's used to make gunpowder. Mix the shit with sulphur and charcoal, add a three percent measure of alcohol to accelerate fermentation and... Boom!"

Boom?

"By royal decree dating back to the 1500s, all the pigeon poop in England legally belongs to the king or queen, in order to protect against redneck rebels blowing up Big Ben."

Big Ben?

"Here in the U.S. right-wing redneck Reverends set on overthrowing the government claim it's their Constitutional right to possess guano."

Max was curious, but…"Sorry, folks, I'm out of real time for crime detection," he announced. "Tune in next real time for further developments in *Case of a Misguided Juvenile Hero*. Until then, this is Yourrrs Truly, Maximo Morgannn a/k/a The Fat Mannn, signing off.

♫Dum-dum dum-dum, dum!♫

Though anxious to know what was going on at the other end of the row of Mr. Quickie workstations, Max—feeling compelled as if by instinct to answer the dinner bell ringing inside his head—got up from his desk and headed for home.

FRIDAY
April 15, 2022

CHAPTER SIXTEEN

Max stopped in his tracks, stunned by sight of a large banner hung above the Mr. Quickie Main Street entrance:

COMING SOON
Branch Office of Tom Owsley
Private Investigations

Inside the copy shop, he looked left for Quickie, but no soap. He swiveled his head right and…On a blank wall at the end of the row of workstation cubicles, another large sign displayed Owsley's big fat half-awake face and slogan:

We sleep with one eye open.

Max hotfooted past his own workstation and other small cubicles toward a large one equipped with computers for multiple users and…Again, he stopped in his tracks, this time at sight of the kid, sitting with ordinary-shod feet propped up at a large desk, talking into a phone.

"…breakthrough last night," the young smartass was saying as Max entered the over-sized space. "Case is sewed up tight as a nun's purse."

An open cardboard box sitting on a table was marked FOOTWEAR. In addition to backward facing *Switcheroos* and an even odder set of high-tops shaped like the feet of a large bird, the box contained a pair of hoofers that in fact resembled… He picked one up, turned it over, and sure enough: a horseshoe was nailed to the sole.

"Righto, Boss. Paperwork will be done in time for today's big event."

Max peeked into another box marked DISGUISES. There he saw wigs of different colors, a monocle, other spectacles and several rubber noses of different sizes and shapes; all new-and-improved gear such as no doubt used by the Oklahoma Bureau of Investigation, except…Yeah, "Old Reliable"—lensless specs with attached black eyebrows, plastic nose and mustache—seemed to still be standard issue at the OSBI.

"So how do you like the digs, Mr. Maximo? High-intensity interrogation lighting and a lie detector have not been installed yet, but…"

"Sorry to rain on your parade kid," said Max, "but you've lifted your leg on the wrong suspect in your very first lay without my instruction. Take it from Yours Truly, there's no hanky-panky—past, present or future—between Mr. Crowe and Mrs. Haggard, who is an odorless angel of mercy."

"'Fraid you're wrong about that, Bro. We have a witness who… By the way, what happened to your ear?"

Max brushed off the kid's dodge. Who was the witness? What did the stool pigeon have to say?

The kid refused to name a name, but copped to obtaining a statement from a Mrs. Crowe companion, who supposedly had a sharp eye and a…

"You really ought to put on a fake ear to cover that unsightly swollen one, Mr. Maximo."

Max demanded to see proof of the statement. In response, the kid shrugged, took a couple of pages of paper from a dest drawer, and handed them over. Max plopped into a chair beside the desk and commenced to read what looked to be a so-called transcript of so-called testimony of a so-called witness:

CLIENT:
Tell this young man what you overheard, Cassie. Repeat exactly what you told me about Bill and…

WITNESS:
Bill-and-Coo. Bill-and-Coo. Time: two-thirty. Conditions: mostly cloudy. Chances of rain…

CLIENT:
Cassandra likes to watch TV, the weather forecasts especially, and of course Sesame Street. She loves Bert.

WITNESS:
Bert-and-Bill.   Bill-and-Coo.   Bert-loves-Bill-loves-Coo. #@!?>**&%#!!! that cheating S.O.B.*

Max looked up from the transcript. "This so-called testimony is hearsay that does not incriminate Bill Crowe and Coo Haggard of hanky-panky," he firmly stated. "The stool pigeon who spilled these beans may have overheard, say, a cuc<u>koo</u> clock in the background, and mistook what the bird was saying for a certain person's nickname. And her foul language is typical of the kind of shady character whose testimony is not fit to be believed."

"We have documentary evidence corroborating the hearsay," said the kid, with a self-satisfied smirk. "Mrs. Haggard sent a love note to Mr. Crowe, written in her own hand."

How would the kid know about Coo Haggard's misinterpretable private message? He must have found Homer. What a break for his own case, Max was thinking...

"The note must have fallen off the leg of one of Mr. Crowe's pigeons, Mr. Maximo. Your old postal service buddy and the unscented 'angel of mercy' have been swapping their homing birds back-and-forth in an attempt to keep their illicit correspondence secret. Mr. Owsley has seen hundreds of cases like this as an OSBI investigator. And as you may recall, in *Case of The Telltale Pigeon Feathers*, Dr. Watson doped out that foreign spies..."

Max demanded to see the note with his own eyes. In response, the kid again shrugged, again reached into a desk drawer, and took out a small metallic capsule, but ... "Sorry, Mr. Maximo," he said, removing a small piece of paper from the container. "Can't let actual evidence out of my mitts — one of Mr. Owsley's strict rules called 'Maintaining Chain of Possession' — but for you, I'll read the smoking gun.

"'Bill, I hate you,'" the kid read aloud. "'I only pretended to be friendly in order to co-train our birds and learn your racing strategy secrets.' The sender of the note, signs off by writing…"

"Aha! The innocent 'pigeon talk' proves <u>no</u> hanky-panky!" said Max. And though it was hard to believe Coo Haggard could hate anyone, he silently noted to himself that the note also eliminated spousal jealousy as a Donald Haggard motive for foul play against Bill Crowe's pigeon. But…

"Just a passing lovers spat, according to Mr. Owsley," said the kid. "Does the sign-off—'Coochie Coochie Coo. Guess who?'—sound like innocent 'pigeon talk' to you, Mr. Maximo?"

No, not exactly, he had to admit to himself, but…"For crying out loud, kid, have you yourself never played the innocent game of Postman's Knock, sometimes called 'Post Office'?"

"No, not that I…"

"Listen and learn."

Max commenced to pass on to the green-as-grass wannabe P.I. the lesson he himself had learned at a thirteenth birthday party his mom had hosted in his honor. Balloons were blown up, paper stringers were hung, cake was served by a professional party planner, who then organized a game in which girls were sent to a bedroom. Boys took turns knocking on the bedroom door to deliver "letters". A randomly chosen girl would open the door and either…

"OMG, you are talking about the old boys-and-girls kissing game. Gross!"

"Well, yeah, some guys got a peck on the cheek. Or you got a 'Return to Sender' card. Then and there I set my cap to someday become a mailman and maybe get…The point is that flirty notes passed back and forth don't mean hanky-panky was ever afoot between Mrs. Haggard and my client."

"Mr. Owsley's open eye sees it differently, but…In case your client's wayward pigeon is still missing and may have met with foul play, there's a P.S. to the note that might have something to do with your case, Mr. Maximo," said the kid, returning his attention to the scrap of paper. "It tends to be what Mr. Owsley calls 'self serving' and therefore not necessarily reliable, but anyway, it says:

"'P.S. I happen to know that Dodo Vogel has always been the 'other woman' in your life. She would do anything to either get you back from Penelope or get back at you.'"

Dodo Vogel? Oh yeah, she was the friendly blonde who cut-in on Bill and Donald Haggard during the FFF pigeon dance and…"Aha! That's evidence that your own client, Mrs. Crowe, had reason to waylay her husband's prize pigeon in a fit of jealousy. There are laws against knee-capping birds without a license."

"Are you kidding, Mr. Maximo? The only reason our client hired us to prove her husband's hanky-panky is to grease the skids of a divorce. She wants to get at what's left of their marital assets before your client loses everything on a big bet. More than anyone else, Mrs. Crowe was hoping her hubby's prize pigeon would win today's Dixie Classic."

Hmmm. Max got up from the kid's over-sized desk. Walking back to his own small cubicle, he silently admitted to himself that the plot of *Case of a Misguided Juvenile Hero* seemed to have thinned down to a single new suspect: the flirtatious blonde bombshell known as Dodo Vogel.

CHAPTER SEVENTEEN

Looking into a vanity table mirror, Dodo applied an extra-long fake eyelash. Yesterday, she had felt much like the Virgin Mary must have felt after the Holy Ghost appeared to her in the form of a pigeon. No, not pregnant, thank God; but confused. Now she understood why Bill had seemed somewhat stand-offish during their dance at the FFF affair; Penelope was in attendance with that squawking bird perched on her shoulder, watching their every move. His current wife's jealous possessiveness also explained why Bill had chosen such a roundabout way of wooing her, she now also understood. But how to respond?

In a flash of divine inspiration, one of her hopelessly romantic mottos had come to her as if on wings of a dove: "Let your love go free. If it comes back it's yours forever. If it does not return…"

Buzz. Buzz. Buzzzzz…

Dodo got up from the vanity, tightened the sash of her bathrobe, and went to the front door.

Like a bat out of hell, in barged Mrs. Ruby Keller, mother of the bride at Wednesday's wedding.

"Things didn't work out between Kandi and Grady," the ex-client announced, before plopping herself down on one of the living room love seats. "And it has not been forty-eight hours since they tied the knot."

Dodo remained standing. How many times would she have to explain to ex-clients? She was a professional wedding planner, not a marriage counselor. Nevertheless, "The course of true love never runs smoothly," she advised.

"Neither do most of that Chevy van's ators."

"Ators?"

"Accelerator, alternator, radiator; you name it. Kandi's ex, that no account Wayne 'Deal-a-Day' Dean, unloaded a lemon in their divorce. Grady wants him to take her back."

Hmmm.

"And Wayne's's willing to make a deal, which got me to thinking: Ms. Vogel, you owe us a refund."

"My dear, Mrs. Keller, the wedding's 'until death does them part' clause only applies to the bride's contract with the groom. I cannot make even an overnight guarantee of outcome. The course of untrue love also runs…"

"That pigeon poop ruined Kandi's almost new denim outfit!"

"Murphy happens."

"And there must have been bad shrimp in that all-you-can eat buffet that came as part of your One-Night Stand honeymoon special at the Fountainblue Motel."

Ah, right on cue, Butch Junior came into the living room.

"Excuse me, Mom, but the more I think about it, the more I think we should tell Mr. Crowe what we did after I flighted one of his racing cocks by mistake. The Dixie Classic results will be coming in within hours and…"

"Later, Butch Junior. Tell Mrs. Keller about the birds and bees. "

"Aw, Mom."

Dodo coaxed from her bashful seventeen-year-old son a repeated explanation of the sometimes unpleasant facts of life, specifically that pigeons' mating instincts and digestive functions were both driven by heartbeats as rapid as 150 to 600 beats per minute.

"In other words, Kandi was no doubt excited to be on her honeymoon," she herself explained to the mother of the understandably embarrassed bride. "She should not have over-indulged in the all-you-can-eat buffet. I cannot be held responsible for, uh, Murphy happening. But for Kandi's next wedding…"

"As a matter of fact, Wayne is willing to take Kandi back," said the concerned mother, rising from the love seat, "but not the Chevy van payments. If her marriage to Grady and divorce from Wayne can't be annulled amiably—Wayne Dean is a chronic dickerer—she has her heart set on wearing that semi-white, semi-indecent dress of yours, at a discounted price that includes no pigeons!"

Deeply moved by the example of true love overcoming marriage and divorce that so closely mirrored her own experience in progress, Dodo agreed to let Kandi wear her dress—for a wedding ceremony only—and showed the mother-of-the-bride-to-again-be to the door. To Butch Junior, she said, "You should be in school. I will handle the matter of Mr. Crowe's racing cock."

Returned to her bathroom, Dodo happened to glance out a window and…That fat man she met at the FFF wingding was standing in the backyard, looking at Butch Junior's pigeon loft. They had more or less made a date to go to the Adventure District in Oklahoma City on Sunday, she recalled, but now… How typical that when *beaus* rained, they poured. What was she to do?

♫*I'm just a girl who cain't say no/ I'm in a terrible fix…* ♫

Remembrance of an old song took Dodo back to being cast—the student-director called it "type casting"—as a character called Ado Annie in a high school production of *Oklahoma!*

♫*I always say, "c'mon let's go/ just when I oughta say nix!* ♫

In the musical play, she had been unable to choose between affections for a traveling peddler, who promised to take her to paradise, and a cute cowboy, who gave her presents.

♫*What you goin' to do when a feller gits flirty/ and starts to talk purty/ What you goin' to do?* ♫

And the boy who played the rug seller was fat, like one of her rock idols, Meatloaf.

♫*I'm just a girl who cain't say no/ cain't seem to say it at all/ I hate to disserpoint a beau…* ♫

Now the new fat man in her life was crossing the backyard toward the kitchen door.

♫...*when a beau is payin' a call!"*

Knock. Knock. Knock.

Just in case the downside of her hopelessly romantic motto—"If your love does not return, it was not meant to be"—turned out to be true, Dodo loosened the sash of her bathrobe and went to the door.

"Maximo Morgan. We met at the FFF shindig and…"

"Why, yes, Max," said Dodo, brightly smiling and slightly batting her newly lashed eyelid. "How nice of you to drop by. Come in and make yourself comfortable on a love seat. I'll warm up a slice of my cherry pie for you."

Another of Dodo's mottos was not to count on roosters until they crowed "I cock-o-doodle do".

CHAPTER EIGHTEEN

Max ankled out the front door of Dodo Vogel's cozy nest, vaguely feeling like a character in a podcast not titled *A Maximo Morgan Mystery.*

Before knocking on the blonde bombshell's back door, he had given her pigeon coop a once-over, repeatedly calling out "Here, Homer, come to Daddy". No soap.

On a love seat inside her nook, he had downed a slice of her cherry pie and grilled her. After at first claiming not to be a "kiss-and-tell" kind of dame, bingo; the friendly babe admitted she had been and still was involved in hanky-panky with his client, Bill Crowe.

Even so, the doll had then batted one of her baby blues and cooed that his own date with her to visit the Oklahoma City Adventure District on Sunday was still on, depending on how "the competition" turned out later today.

Obviously, the naive skirt had been referring to the Dixie Classic pigeon race. Obviously, she was not in the know that Bill's prize bird, Homer, was out of commission and had missed the trip to the Birmingham, Alabama starting line. And though he had already had the adventure of touring the American Pigeon Museum, he had not been to the Oklahoma City zoo since its capture of a new elephant. So, with a gut feeling the dame's other squeeze, Crowe, would be out of the picture by Sunday, he had played along.

Now at the wheel of the parked boiler, Max took off his mailman's cap and scratched his head. The hamster inside his noggin began to spin a wheel. *Case of a Misguided Juvenile Hero* was practically a blow-by-blow replay of Sam Spade's *Case of The Maltese Falcon*, he fully realized.

Like the devious Brigid O'Shaughnessy a/k/a "Miss Wonderly" who ankled into Spade's office and got the gullible gumshoe to track down what she thought was a valuable bird statue, Bill Crowe had played on their USPS buddyship to con him into searching for Homer. And like the *femme fatale* in Spade's case, Crowe was not a straight shooter. Mom was right: a guy who would cheat in the marriage game would cheat at anything. Such as a high-stakes pigeon race. Especially if he had a bad bet riding on the outcome.

Spade fell for the good-looking *femme fatale* like a tipped-over stack of dirty dishes, and took the case. Hours later, not by coincidence, his partner got bumped off. Spade was no Boy Scout—he was involved in hanky-panky with his partner's Missus—but eventually…"When a man's partner is killed he's supposed to do something about it," the hardboiled dick had the decency to realize. "It doesn't make any difference what you thought of him. He was your partner and you're supposed to do something about it."

Yeah, in the end, Spade—though dame-dizzy for the O'Shaughnessy broad—called his cop buddy, Pat Chambers; and sent the *femme fatale*—his own client—to the Big House for a long stretch in stir, if not a long stretch of her neck at the business end of a hangman's rope.

Max put on his cap, fired up the boiler, put pedal to the metal, and headed for downtown.

Sam Spade's famous case was never mainly about finding a bird statue that turned out to be worthless, he now realized. At its core, *Case of The Maltese Falcon* was always about a hardboiled P.I.'s struggle between turning in his own client—which might cost him his gumshoe license—or doing the right thing.

Ten minutes later, Max parked the boiler and ankled toward the town's police station. The local Chief Five-O—a guy named Potter—was no Pat Chambers. He was a typical do-nothing donutter who wore the badge for the perks that went with it. They'd had multiple run-ins through the years, but...

"Hey, Chief," he hollered to the uniformed paper-pusher, sitting at a desk as usual, "got a delicate lay on my hands that calls for official police action, ASAP!"

"Go away, Morgan. I'm up to my ears in paperwork."

Max ignored the attempted brush-off, sat down in a chair beside the desk, and laid out the facts of *Case of a Misguided Juvenile Hero*. In conclusion, "When one of a guy's oldest and best friends goes missing under suspicious circumstances, a guy is supposed to do something about it, Potter. It doesn't matter that the only suspect is his client. A guy is duty-bound to call the cops."

"So you have, uh, slimmed down from imitating that oldtime radio fat man to playing Ace Ventura," said the flatfoot, echoing the sarcastic tone the kid had used in dissing the famous pet detective. "A step in the right career direction, to judge by the look of that ear. Take your 'case' to the U.S. Wildlife Bureau, ASAP!"

Hmmm.

Max took off his cap, scratched his head, and...It hit him like a heavy drop of pigeon poop onto his sore ear. *Case of a Misguided Juvenile Hero* was a lot like Ventura's *Case of When Nature Calls*.

In that Ventura adventure a couple of Brit diplomats hired the famous pet detective to track down, not a valuable racing pigeon but a sacred Great White bat that was needed for a wedding of African aristocrats to seal a peace treaty between tribes. Sort of like Americans releasing pigeons at such ceremonies, Max imagined. Turned out that Ventura's own clients had set up Ace to be the fall guy for their own involvement in batnapping. They wanted to queer the wedding, and the peace deal, in order to get their mitts on the country's bat caves that contained tons of guano worth billions of bucks as fertilizer.

"So what are you saying, Morgan?" said Potter. "You want me to bust your client for attempting to corner the local pigeon poop market?"

Hmmm.

Max recalled a placard at the pigeon museum saying that pigeon poop was once a highly valued source of something called saltpeter that was used to make gunpowder.

Hmmm.

He also now recalled Ranger Mortimer saying that all pigeon droppings in England were by law owned by kings and queens because of their potential to be fermented by radical right-wing rednecks set on overthrowing the government.

Hmmm.

The U.S. Wildlife Bureau expert also referred to radical right-wing rednecks in the Okmulgee County as "Reverends", and…

Hmmm.

In the post office Rubber Room, Nelson Strauser accused Bill Crowe of being a so-called Reverend! And Mom said so too.

Hmmm?

It hit him in the face like the blast of an exploding cigar! Dozens if not hundreds of racing pigeons would be returning to Okmulgee County from Birmingham, Alabama, within hours, no doubt loaded with fermented saltpeter!

"Call me if you hear a loud boom," the town's Chief do-nothing donutter yelled, as Max bolted out the door of police headquarters.

CHAPTER NINETEEN

Coo drove her pickup into a field north of her lofts and parked it in a copse of trees, not only to get the vehicle out of the way of Bert's fellow Reverends who continued to arrive at their farm. Her husband had become increasingly menacing in manner since her return from seeing Bill Crowe at the post office yesterday. He must have in fact intercepted the flirtatious message attached to the leg of Bill's prize racer, she reckoned. Upon Princess Kasmir's return from Birmingham, she herself would stealthily take flight, no matter what the outcome of the Oklahoma bracket of the Dixie Classic proved to be.

Out of the truck, she looked at her watch; then up to the sky, where Donald continued to ominously circle. The Princess should be more than halfway across Arkansas by now, hopefully flying faster than the hundreds of other pigeons returning to Okmulgee County. With fingers crossed, Coo trudged on foot back toward her lofts and Bert's barn.

Today was the 15th of April, three days prior to the anniversary date of the start of Paul Revere's famous midnight ride, but a Friday, which she imagined must be the reason militia members had pushed up their annual celebration and were now hooting-and-hollering inside the barn. Several of them were pigeon trainers and racers with birds entered in the Grand Prix, and even Bert—a pigeon hater—had seemed to somewhat favorably notice the coincidence of events.

In the kitchen earlier, her virtually illiterate spouse had worn an unusually excited-seeming smirk while reciting a memorized stanza of the famous poem beginning, "Listen, my children, and you shall hear/ Of the midnight ride of Paul Revere…"

He had chanted, "'Then his friend climbed to the tower of the church/ Up the wooden stairs with a stealthy tread/ To the belfry-chamber over-head/ And startled the pigeons from their perch!'"

Now, from inside the barn… ♫**West bound and down/ loaded up and truckin'/ We gonna do what they say can't be done** ♫ the rowdy and already drunken Reverends loudly sang. ♫**We've got a long way to go/ and a short time to get there/ We're west bound/ just watch ol Bandit run…** ♫

Hmmm. "Bandit" was the name of a Reverend's prize pigeon entered in the Dixie Classic, and . . Other altered lyrics of the old redneck anthem seemed to be about… ♫**We've loaded up ol' Skeeter 's cock/ he'll be unloadin' on Little Rock…** ♫

Coo ran to the barn, pressed an ear to one of its raw wooden walls and…

"Say Skeeter," one of the militia members inside the barn shouted, "any word yet from Cousin Cooter?"

"Yeah, Skeeter, the Okmulgee County Brigade ought to've unloaded on the Capitol by now," someone else shouted.

"Hold your water, boys. I've got static on the line."

♫**West bound and down/ loaded up and truckin'/ We gonna do what they say can't be done…** ♫

Like a few other Reverends, Bert was originally from Arkansas. She had thought that connection—along the Little Rock setting of the movie *Daddy and Them* that featured "their' song about "biting our noses right off of our faces"—must have been the reason the brute had recently stuck a poster for the movie on a wall of his barn "man cave". Together with a souvenir postcard showing the domed Arkansas State Capitol that was almost a dead ringer for the U.S. Capitol in Washington, D.C.

♫**We've got a long way to go/ and a short time to get there…** ♫

It dawned on Coo also that as a crow—or flock of pigeons—flew, Little Rock, Arkansas was on a straight line from Birmingham, Alabama to Henryetta, Oklahoma.

🎵**We've loaded up ol' Skeeter's cock/ he'll be unloadin' on Little Rock…** 🎵

"Hold on, boys! I've got Cooter back on the line and…"

"What's he say, Skeeter? Was a boom heard 'round the world?"

"Shit! Or rather, no shit hit the fan! Cooter says the Capitol is still standin' like a bosomy virgin's tit."

"Dang it, the Arkansas National Guard must have shot down the Brigade. Poor Bandit; he was a patriotic American hero that oughta be stuffed-and-mounted."

"Nope. Cooter says there was no anti-aircraft fire in Little Rock today."

"Dang it, I knew that QAnon recipe for three percent *Jack Daniel* was not enough to ferment the pigeon poop."

Jack Daniel Whiskey? Ferment pigeon poop?!

Coo dashed around a corner of the barn, kicked open a door, stormed inside and shouted: "What have you sons-of-bitches done to Princess Kasmir?!"

Most of the sorry bunch shrank back from her, including Bert. But then, "No need to get your underwear in a bunch, Coo," he said, smirking of course. "Reverends in Alabama gave your Princess and all the other Okmulgee County pigeons a hearty meal before starting the big race, but Skeeter's cousin says nothin'…"

"Hearty meal! Pigeons are not to be fed for at least twenty-four hours before a race. And *Jack Daniel?* That's whiskey! Alcohol could cause…"

"Yeah, fermentation of the saltpeter in their poop," said one of the Reverends. "The bombs were supposed to be dropped on the U.S. Capitol over in Arkansas to start a revolution, but the dang recipe…"

"QAnon's never wrong. *Kaopectate* in the mix to get the bombers across Tennessee must've been overdone by those yahoos over in Alabama," said another of the right-wing redneck militiamen. "Constipation must've threw off the timing of the attack."

"Holy shit, Skeeter! That means the Okmulgee County Brigade is still west bound and down, loaded up an'… truckin' for home!"

"Scatter, boys! Every Reverend for himself!"

Coo followed the panicked mob out of the barn. All the Reverends except Bert ran for parked trucks, each equipped with a gun rack, each emblazoned with images of Confederate flags and/or bumper stickers saying *Don't Tread On Me*…. *Ride With Reverends*…*When You Elect Clowns Expect a Circus*…and the like.

She looked upward. Soon, God willing, Princess Kasmir—overfed, possibly under the influence of alcohol, and constipated—would be coming in on a wing-and-a-prayer. But Donald was on the loose and…No, thank God, she saw the pigeon predator in the distance, flying away and…

Coo's hopefully last ever sight of Bert Haggard was the big bully running toward the farm's hilly south forty.

CHAPTER TWENTY

Max stood at a living room window. Warily, he pulled back a curtain an inch or two. Figuratively speaking, he kicked himself. His touting of the American Pigeon Museum had led his mom to suggest to her new gentleman friend an outing to the Oklahoma City Adventure District.

Figuratively speaking, he fetched another foot to his backside. For a planned podcast of *A Maximo Mystery* installment, he had again borrowed Mom's cell phone. So he had been out of touch with her for hours, unable to warn his mom of the impending…

Max again looked at his watch. Okmulgee County pigeons loaded with fermented saltpeter would be completing their homing flights in the Oklahoma Bracket of the Dixie Classic within the next half hour. And there was nothing more he could do about it.

After hotfooting from the police station, he had raced home, urgently intending to sound the alarm, but…No one at the County Sheriff's Department had returned from lunch. Only machines had picked up his calls to the Oklahoma National Guard Headquarters and Governor's Office, and no one from either place had got back to him. Following a late lunch and short nap on the living room sofa, he had finally gotten through to Colonel Mortimer at the U.S. Wildlife Bureau, but…

"Remain calm and carry on," the Colonel had advised. "Do not; I repeat, do <u>not</u> cause civilian panic by spreading personal panic!" Seeking shelter ASAP and prayer were the best courses of action when confronted with carpet bombing by superior forces, the pigeon expert had advised before abruptly ending the call.

So there he stood, semi-sheltered and prayerful that his mom would get back from OKC safely before…Again Max looked at his watch. Figuratively speaking, he again…Thank God, his mom's gentleman friend's worn out old *Willis* wood-paneled *Jeepster* skidded to a stop out front.

Max hotfooted from the house and across the lawn. At the curb, "Are you sure you won't come in for pie, Vernon?" Mom was saying after getting out of the antique vehicle. As the old "Woodie" sped away, he grabbed hold of her arm and dragged her toward the parked boiler.

Headed for downtown, "I don't think Vernon much enjoyed our date," Mom said. "He doesn't like pigeons and wanted to go to the horse racing track. But he forgot to bring his wallet and, well, you know how I feel about betting on animal races. We went to the zoo, but the monkeys. . ."

"Mom, you were right all along about Bill Crowe," Max blurted, before putting his mother wise to what was afoot, or rather to what was awing.

"Maxie, I hope you are not 'A-S-S-U-Ming'," she fretted.

The only safe place within quick striking distance was the town hall basement, where citizens hunkered during threats of tornados, but…Only when he turned a corner and saw banners strung across Main Street did Max recall that the Governor was scheduled to pass through town, which likely explained the timing of the Reverends' pigeon attack. Downtown was crowded with potential victims.

After circling a block…What the heck—desperate situations required desperate actions—he parked the boiler in front of a fire hydrant.

Arrived at town hall on foot with Mom…Uh oh, someone must have put public safety at risk by spreading personal panic. Though not seeming to be overly alarmed—some inside the town hall lobby were even laughing—the joint was jammed with potential victims seeking refuge.

Max peeked into the Town Council chamber and…thankfully, an emergency command center was being set up.

A large but portable electronic board had been placed next to the elevated podium where the Council Chairlady usually presided. Colored lights began to flash. Letters and numbers like the abbreviated names of teams in big league baseball games began to appear. "Look, Honey," a fella beside him said to a dame on his arm, "that's our loft, 'PDQ'. It won't be long until the birds start clocking-in."

A guy standing beside the board put a bullhorn to his face and shouted, **"People with powerful electronic devices turned on or powerful magnets in your possession, please move to the back of the chamber! You're interfering with signals from the landing pads."**

Moving with his mom in that direction, Max was surprised to see Bill Crowe backed against the wall, twitching and sweating like a man about to be shot by a firing squad.

"Feeling remorrrse about what 'happened' to Homer?" he said to the right-wing Reverend.

"Yeah, I've got eleven other cocks in the race, but Homer was my best shot at winning Grand Prix money," his ex-buddy answered, with a nervous jerk of his head and shoulders. "I was counting on you to track him down, Max, but you failed to deliver the goods."

Failed to track down and deliver the misguided juvenile hero! Bullroar! Maximo Morgan always got the...

"Citizens of Henryetta!" said someone through the chamber's loud speaker system. **"Remain calm and carry on."**

Max wheeled around and...What in the name of Mike! Up on the Chairlady's podium stood none other than that private dick...

"My name is Tom Owsley. I am a Special Agent of the Oklahoma State Bureau of Investigation. For the past several weeks, I have been sleeping undercover in this community with one eye open, investigating suspected tampering in this year's Dixie Classic by right-wing extremists.

Ohhhhh...the assembled citizens moaned.

"Stay calm. The Bureau dangled the Governor as bait, and I am happy to report that hundreds of constipated pigeons were today detained without incident after crossing the Arkansas border."

Ohhhhhhhh…

"Stay calm. I am unhappy to report that a few stragglers, believed to be based in and around your town, made it through the Bureau's checkpoints."

Ohhhhhhhhhhh….

"Stay calm and carry on!"

"What about my prize hen, Fredda?" someone shouted.

"What about my prize cock, Roberto?" someone else hollered.

Right on cue, letters and a number in a second column appeared on the electronic board.

"What the hell, it's Bill Crowe's prize cock that's clocked-in!" someone yelled.

Ohhhhhh…

"Homer's posted the fastest speed!"

Ohhhhhh…

"Homer's gonna win the Dixie Classic!

Ohhhhhh…

Max turned and saw that Bill Crowe, with jaw dropped and ears twitching, looked to be stunned by the posted result. More stunned when a semi-familiar lanky dark-haired dame with a redheaded parrot on her shoulder rushed at him and kissed his cheek. And even more stunned when Owsley appeared beside him and said:

"William Crowe, you are hereby charged with conspiracy to tamper with an accredited interstate pigeon race and attempted overthrow of government in the United States."

Ohhhhhh…

"I'm innocent of tampering!" Crowe howled. "Wait 'til Coo Haggard's prize Princess Kasmir clocks-in. Her flight is ten miles longer. Her average speed may be faster. Coo Haggard did the tampering."

Ohhhhhh…

"The Reverends are just good ol' boys, never meanin' no harm," he wailed. "We were just funnin'."

Ohhhhhh…

"Mr. Maximo," said the kid, suddenly beside him, "I was used as a clueless cat's-paw in Mr. Owsley's undercover investigation against your client. I thought it was a case of domestic hanky-panky; not domestic terrorism."

"He's a good kid, Morgan," said Owsley, "and beginning to wise-up to how the cookie crumbles. Take him back. Give him another chance to jot for you."

Bang! Bang! Bang!

"Hold the phone!"

Bang! Bang! Bang!

It was the Town Council Chairlady, banging her gavel and screaming into the podium microphone.

"Yes, the pigeon known as '1632' clocked-in first, but at the wrong loft! The cock is hereby impeached!"

Ohhhhhhhhh…

Into the back wall cluster next came none other than Dodo Vogel, with a pigeon in her hands. "Here, Bill; here's Homer," she said, holding out the previously missing bird. "I sent him to Birmingham, Alabama for you, but he returned to Homewrecker in Butch Junior's loft, with my hopelessly romantic answer to your hopelessly romantic note."

Ohhhhhhhhh…

"Homewrecker!" shouted the lanky dark-haired dame, lunging at Dodo and clawing the babe's blonde hair. "Homewrecker!" the redheaded parrot on the attacker's shoulder screeched.

Ohhhhhhhhh…

Max glanced downward to confirm… Yeah, his mom was wearing her magnetized *Magno Mocs*.

"Stand back!" he shouted. "That heroic juvenile bird is loaded and could be set off by a magnetic field at any moment!"

Ohhhhhhhhh…

To Dodo Vogel, he cooed, "Hand over the pigeon, Dollface. Nice and easy, hand over Homer."

Ohhhhhhhhh…
With bird in hand to finally close *Case of a Misguided Juvenile Hero*, Max shuffled slowly and carefully toward the Town Council chamber exit. Almost to the door…He heard no loud boom, but sure enough…Oh well, in the famous words of Robert E. Lee: Sometimes a guy's the pigeon; sometimes the statue.
Ohhhhhhhhhhhhhh!

THE
END

HUMBLE PIE

WILLIAM LEROY

Library of Congress Cataloguing-in-Publication Data

LeRoy, William [1.17.2023]

Humble Pie: A Maximo Morgan Mystery
by William LeRoy

p. cm
ISBN 979-8-9869494-2-0

1. Humor—Fiction.
2. Oklahoma, United States—Fiction.
3. Culinary Arts—Fiction.
4. Mystery—Fiction.
I. Title

10 9 8 7 6 5 4 3 2 1

Manufactured in the United States of America
First Edition

WLR/MB

A Maximo Morgan Mystery
HUMBLE PIE
WILLIAM LEROY

MONDAY

June 2, 2022

CHAPTER ONE

At his workstation inside Mr. Quickie's copy shop, Max adjusted alignment of desk plaques identifying him by name as Maximo Morgan, and by game as Private Investigations. In fact, he had no gumshoe cases to work. And due to a recent onslaught of applications for absentee voter ballots by Mayor Bailey, the stamper he used to notarize signatures in return for Quickie letting him occupy the workstation was currently out for repair. Except for the plaques, his platter was bare.

Also discouraging was a recent article in *Private Dick Database* about crime rates in smallish towns. A burg called Bogalusa down in Louisiana had sixty-five yearly crimes per one thousand residents; almost twenty of them violent, no doubt including multiple murders. In his territory, however, the same-size nearby county seat community of Okmulgee, Oklahoma, had only about fifty annual crimes per thousand people, only six or seven of which were bloody.

Max again sighed. No doubt P.I. prospects were even bleaker in the more immediate vicinity of his hometown private dicking grounds of Henryetta, Oklahoma. But he still lived with his mother, and Mom had no tolerance for itching caused by mosquitos such as infested Louisiana, so…

Light from overhead dimmed. Max looked up. Hovering over him was the umbrella-size brim of what must have been a forty-gallon cowboy hat… on the head of…

Standing at the desk was none other than Mr. O.B. Everheart, a cattle baron known to be the richest man in the county.

"Mind if I squat?" said the aged baron, slowly lowering himself into a chair. "This dry spell we're havin' makes my old bones ache more than usual. The wind is up too," he said, before continuing with delivery of a lengthy weather commentary. But then…

"Didn't this here little sign used to say 'Confidentiality Guaranteed?'"

"Absolutely," Max replied, reaching into a drawer for a third plaque that spelled out the professional guarantee. "Been so busy lately I had to make room for the paperwork, all of which was strictly confidential and has since gone into the shredderrr."

"Well, I'm not one to bother a body who's busy," said the possibly potential P.I. client, slowly rising from the chair.

"No bother, Mr. Everheart. I just recently wrapped up the highly confidential *Case of A Misguided Juvenile Hero* for an old postal service buddy named Bill Crowe. Doped out that the client was trying to do the coochie-coo with a coincidentally named Mrs. Coo Haggard, also married to another. I have recorded a podcast about…"

"Well, it's about my wife," said the old codger, again lowering himself. "Honeybee left me with a youngun to raise and…"

"Uh huh, the Missus ran off with a lusty young cowboy, no doubt. Don't worry, Mr. Everheart, I'll track 'em down and…"

"Actually, Honeybee just up and died of the sugar diabetes almost thirty years ago, right after calving a gal that I went and named Sugar."

Oh.

"At a square dance for lonely hearts, along came Mimi. I met her doin' an allemande-left and, well, shortly afterward we sure enough promenaded home together."

As O.B. Everheart continued with what was sure to be the same old story heard a hundred times before by no doubt all but one hawkshaw from Hoboken, New Jersey to Henryetta, Oklahoma, Max took a small spiral-bound notebook and ballpoint pen from a pocket of his old-fashioned double-breasted suit and commenced to jot.

"I don't know why Mimi picked me out of the herd," said the cattle baron. "I was some older; still am, quite a bit senior as a matter of fact. She said she liked my brand—O.B.E.—that I have stuck on this-and-that, even though it turned out she doesn't care for the company of livestock and won't eat meat. See, Mimi was what they call a debutante who had recently been introduced to overseas high society. Me on the other hand, well, the only beauty contest I've ever been invited to is the annual Fat Stock Show down in Fort Worth. I have tried to make Mimi happy by giving her everything she wanted, but…"

The doting husband went on to say that to make his younger second wife happy he had built the famous over-sized house on the south side of town—"an almost exact copy of that mansion called 'Althorp House' where that Princes Diana Somebody grew up, but without the unneeded bedroom wings"—and cleared out surrounding residents to create a park for deer statues and such. He had gladly paid for the wife's trips to Europe to shop for fancy dresses, jewelry, and such. And had got himself fitted-up for a monkey suit in order to awkwardly host dinner parties with her, but…

"It's been hard for the wife to find suitable people to show up, no doubt because, well, I always knew an old cow puncher like me was not half refined enough for Mimi," the old man said, before bringing a red bandana from a pocket, putting the rag to his big round face and blowing his bulbous warty nose. "Still, I thought she was happy enough, until this morning."

Max leaned forward to hear the predictable ending of the old cow puncher's story, no doubt including receipt of a Dear John letter and demand for a generous divorce settlement.

"I was not eavesdropping," the odd-man-out mumbled, "at least not on purpose. I picked up a downstairs phone to make a call and…and I heard a fella tell Mimi that…that I had to be made to…to disappear."

"Disappear?!"

"Yep, and the wife told the smooth-talker she would see to it before he got into town."

Instinctively, Max put a hand to his chest, just to make sure his Roscoe was holstered inside his jacket and ready for pointing.

"I wouldn't want to hog-tie Mimi; not if she's not happy. So to save her the embarrassment of getting rid of me face-to-face, I just wrote out a note, sayin' I would be hunkerin' out at the ranch."

Max again instinctively checked his Roscoe. Out at a remote home on a range without armed protection, the client would be a sitting duck.

"But after I packed up and headed out there…Dang it, Mr. Morgan, I got to thinkin'. Who knew what sort of fella Mimi's other fella might turn out to be? She might find herself in unexpected danger. I couldn't just walk out on her without…So I just turned around, came back to town and…"

Uh oh. The old guy on the wrong side of a typical so-called love triangle reached into his own jacket pocket, but… brought out what looked to be only a…

"Here you are, Mr. Morgan," O.B. Everheart said, after scribbling into a small booklet and now pushing a slip of paper across the desk. "Just to make sure Mimi stays alright…and happy, I would be obliged if you would keep a confidential private eye on her—and another one on Sugar—for as long as possible after my…my disappearance."

Max grabbed the check without even looking at its amount. Finally, he had his mitts on not only a case to work, but a lay sure to involve at least attempted murrrderrr.

CHAPTER TWO

Mimi Everheart *nee* Goodrich paced toward a grand mahogany staircase at one end of her mansion's grandiose "Hall of Heraldry", above which a large Botsford Family crest was mounted. There, she turned around and paced toward the opposite end of the ninety-foot-long Hall—an enlarged and somewhat enhanced replica of the grand saloon of England's famed Althorp House—where an equally large and even more ornate crest of her maternal Goodrich Family was displayed above a grand fireplace.

Beneath a balcony along one side wall, numerous other insignia denoted other lines of her ancestry. Hanging beneath a matching balcony on the other side, however, was simply an heroic scale portrait of Princess Diana, unaccompanied, alas, by any crest linking Mimi to the Princess' noble albeit non-royal Spencer Family.

On an antique console beneath the portrait, a smudged wine glass sat next to a sheet of paper emblazoned with the United Kingdom's royal coat of arms.

Mimi had begun to think of herself as upper-crust at age eight while watching Princess Di's wedding on TV. And in fact, she might well have been born a princess or at least a duchess if not for her foolish mother who—though presented as a debutante at the Court of Versailles—had returned to America to marry a local haberdasher.

Nevertheless, Mimi had diligently studied her genealogy. She had traced her lineage back to American colonial times, specifically to a sixth great-grandfather: a British loyalist named

Amos Botsford, which made her an honorary Daughter of King George III but, alas, still an untitled commoner.

Even so, she might have become a princess like Di by marriage, or at least a viscountess if her so-called high school friend, Mamie Motley, had not disgraced herself and sister debutantes during the Camelot Ball of 1992 in London. The overly eager little tramp had inexcusably made a laughing stock of the entire delegation of American *Kraft Cheese* debs by allowing herself to be seduced by a mere London Court Hotel waiter!

As a result, she herself had come home unbetrothed; forced by circumstances to wed only a low-born "cattle baron", O.B. Everheart, who—despite his advanced age—stubbornly refused to voluntarily give up the ghost. Not that her undeserved unseemly marital status would matter after tomorrow, when…

"Pardon, Ms. Everheart," said a housemaid upon entering the Hall. "Movers from the storage company are here to make Princess Diana disappear."

Unable to bear the sight of four ruffians handling the saintly princess, Mimi hurried to the console, picked up the smudged wine glass and sheet of paper; then retreated toward a sitting room. Later today she would find and stick onto the wall a photo of Queen Elizabeth, perhaps flanked by a picture of Her Majesty's odious son-and-heir, but…Mimi ground her teeth. She would go willingly to the gallows before she curtsied to, or otherwise acknowledged legitimacy of that murderous witch, Camilla!

Oh yes, the scheming mistress of the future king had murdered the shoulda-coulda-woulda been rightful future queen; there was no doubt about that. As a charter member of the Sisters of Diana Society, for the past twenty-four years Mimi had diligently researched the circumstances surrounding Di's martyrdom, though the outcome of her efforts had been obvious from the start.

Camilla had the most to gain by Diana's death; hence the most compelling motive to see to it that the beloved Princess-in-exile permanently disappeared in the bowels of a Paris tunnel. Yes,

by then Charles was already legally free to marry the conniving Camilla; but his mother, the Queen—as head of the Church of England—would never have allowed a both divorced-and-unwidowed son to become king, with his homewrecking concubine roosting on the throne beside him.

Equally obvious was the means of murder. Not by car wreck; that was only a cover-up. On no, poison—the most difficult cause of death to later prove—was well known to be a conniving woman's wily way of getting ahead in life. The only wrinkle to iron out was how Camilla had managed to deliver a deadly dose. And during a pilgrimage to England last year…

Arrived at a sitting room desk, Mimi sat down and again read the officious letter a mailman had yesterday insisted on handing to her personally:

CROWN OFFICE of CHANCERY*
Lord Chancellor for Justice

Ms. Goodrich:

By warrant duly issued under the Crown Prerogatives Act*
on the 13th Day of May, 2022, Major Lawrence Jesterson,
O.B.E. (Ret), is authorized to personally present to you his
credentials and Crown tidings of import on behalf of H.R.H.

God Save the Queen!

Selina Norman O.M.G.
Asst. Clerk of Rolls
Lost & Found Dept.

With a sigh, Mimi returned the notice of outstanding warrant to the sitting room desk, next to the smudged wine glass.

During last year's transatlantic pilgrimage she had been disappointed but not surprised to find that the touching London memorial to the People's Princess—put on display inside Harrods department store by the suspicious father of the Egyptian playboy who had been Diana's escort on the night of her tragic demise—had been removed. The Queen was deep into dotage. Her son-and-heir was in the process of taking charge. Behind the curtains at Buckingham Palace, the wicked Camilla was pulling the strings. Only Diana's supposedly dearly

devoted brother, the 9th Earl Spencer, was keeping memory of his divine sibling alive at the family's ancestral home, or so she had thought.

She was therefore both surprised, disappointed and infuriated the next day of her mission upon finding that the gate to the family's Althorp House country estate had been locked. Pilgrims desiring to pay homage to the Earl's sainted sister at the place where she had been permanently laid to rest had been cruelly turned away. Oh yes, obviously Camilla—fearful that Diana's remains would be dug up and autopsied—had put the squeeze on Di's weak-kneed brother. There was no doubt about that.

Not to be denied in her quest to take selfies at her idol's tasteful Grecian memorial and purchase authentic souvenirs in the Althorp House gift shoppe, she had climbed a wrought iron fence and . .

Honk. Honk. Honk.

"That's bound to be the Uber car you ordered," said the housemaid from the sitting room doorway."

Earlier today Mimi had received a phone call from a Major Jesterson, the Crown Office of Chancery official assigned to execute a warrant on behalf of H.R.H. Queen Elizabeth. "Per protocol", he would be arriving at her residence at dawn tomorrow, the major said. And prior to his arrival "with tidings", also per protocol…

Honk. Honk. Honk.

"Tell Sugar to move the lard or she will miss the bus to Tulsa and her Aunt Peg will have eaten all the cake!" she instructed, regarding her almost thirty-year-old overweight stepdaughter who was in the way of tomorrow's reckoning.

Honk. Honk. Honk.

Obviously, Her Majesty's Secret Service wanted no witnesses to her own disappearance, nor could Mimi herself bare the thought of being seen as a common criminal.

Honk. Honk. Honk.

CHAPTER THREE

After polishing off a slice of apple pie *a la mode*, Max ordered a cup of coffee, put his new so-called smart phone on the Wide-O-Wake Cafe counter, and punched a so-called icon. Out of the little electronic box, first came the recorded *clomp, clomp, clomping* sounds of his mom's footsteps…next, her recorded voice saying, *There he goes, into that drugstore. He's stepping onto scales… Cachung…Weight: two hundred and forty-six pounds. Fortune: danger.*

♫Dum dum-dum, dum♫

Whooo is it?

♫Dum dum-dum, dum♫

Maximo Morgan's the name, said his own recorded voice. *Private dicking is my game.*

♫Dum dum-dum, dum♫

I was at my desk, boning up on small town crime rates and wondering where my next meal would come from, when a well known cattle baron limped into Mr. Quickie's copy shop and…

"Hey, Max, do you mind?" said a guy perched on the stool to his left. "I came in for a bowl of chili, not for an old radio soap opera."

Max swiveled slightly to the right and likewise moved the cell phone.

…said his young wife and her slide-trombone side man in a three-piece combo were plotting to make him disappear. I call it Case of the Baron and the Bimbo.

The guy to his right got up from an untouched plate of meatloaf topped with mashed potatoes and ankled out the door without paying his tab.

"Max, for cryin' out loud," said Booger Tubb, the cafe proprietor. "You're my best eater and a valued customer, but your, uh, 'podcasts' are drownin' out the juke box songs and, uh, interferin' with clientele digestion."

Max detected the hint, got up from the stool, and—without leaving his usual fifty cent tip—also ankled out the cafe door.

Dog-gone-it, his gumshoe ambitions dated back to his teenaged years, when he discovered his deceased father's attic stash of pulp case reports, all of which he had proceeded to devour. So he had gained private dickery know-how at a young age, but failed to shed fat and never developed the muscle of a Mike Hammer, a Sam Spade, a Phillip Marlowe, so became a mailman.

During a twenty-five-year career in postal service he had picked up streetwise moxie, and at night studied TV re-runs of cases handled by Joe Mannix, Tom Magnum, Jim Rockford, Adrian Monk, Scooby Doo and the like. With his mom, he had solved and re-solved all the Jessica Fletcher *Murder She Wrote* mysteries, but…

Truth be told, he had been only a kibitzer until stumbling upon a role model in his weight class: Brad Runyon a/k/a The Fat Man, who had gumshoed back in the days of *Noir*.

He had mastered Runyon's baritone drawl. He had suited up in Forties-and-Fifties style duds and two-tone wingtip shoes like Runyon wore. He had set up shop at Mister Quickie's. Cases came along. And about two months ago a junior high school kid—an overweight pear-shaped lookalike of his own teenaged self—had ankled up to his desk. The kid too had studied all the pulp P.I. records from the past. He too had ambition to walk in the flatfootsteps of Hammer, Spade, Marlowe. Not to mention ankle in those of a new current-day personal role model, namely Yours Truly.

The kid had volunteered to be his "Watson"—a jotter of notes and writer of case reports like the guy who made Sherlock Holmes famous—and did in fact help put out a book about *Case of A Puzzling Book*. But the neo-pulp had not hit the bestseller lists, and the kid—not yet knowing c'mere-from-sic'em about the gumshoe game—had taken a powder. Went to work for an Owsley yardbird who slept with one eye closed. Yeah, the kid had come crawling back, wanting a second chance, but...

What the heck, Brad Runyon had personally reported his cases on the radio. Thankfully, eleven of the Fat Man's first-person accounts had been saved on a CD. He had repeatedly listened to all of them of course, from *Case of a Twice-Told Secret* to *Case of a Crooked Horse* to *Case of Murder by Nightmare*. And now, according to the grapevine, audio was back, bigtime, in the form of so-called podcasts, but...

Regretting that he had not cut the kid some slack for a rookie mistake, Max ankled into Quickie's and...Bingo. None other than his ex-Watson had plopped his big be-hind into the chair on the client side of his desk.

"Just dropped by to see how you're getting along, Mr. Maximo. And by the way, in case your mom needs her lawn mowed, well, school's out for the summer, and my dad is after me to get off the bean bag."

"Live-and-learn, kid," Max answered, after plopping his own be-hind into his own jumbo-sized chair. "By lucky coincidence, I just landed a lay with a big fat check for expenses, and could use a scribe. *Case of the Baron and the Bimbo* is a dead ringer for Percy Wilson's *Case of Mister Big Bucks and Miss Big Boobs*, with the makings of also becoming a bestseller."

"Are you saying what I think you're saying, Mr. Maximo?" said the forgiven young jotter, taking a small spiral-bound notebook from a shirt pocket and a pencil from behind a stuck-out ear.

"Yeah, it could turn out to be a case of murrrderrr unless...."

"So what's our play? Call in the cops right away or..."

"Are you kidding, kid? The quickest way to get the client rubbed out would be to involve clueless Barney Fifes. I've got the 'John Doe' laid low, very low, at the Fountainblue Motel."

"Yeah, that's the play Sam Spade made with Brigid O'Shaughnessy in *Case of the Maltese Falcon*. Savvy move, Mr. Maximo."

Max put the kid wise to the facts of the dead ringer as confided by O.B. Everheart, but…

"Hmmm. On its surface, sounds more like *Case of Double Indemnity*," his jotter opined, referring to the famous *Noir* case in which a *femme fatale* conned an insurance salesman to fit her husband into a policy that paid double in case of death by accident; then got cozy with the sucker and conspired with him to stage such an "mishap".

"No way, José. The client has already showered this bimbo with everything money can buy, and she'll likely get at least half of the rest of his fortune by inheritance. This is a love triangle set-up, not an insurance scam."

"Maybe, but you know what that U.S. Marshal said in *Case of The Fugitive*."

"Remind me."

"The savvy lawman said the prominent doctor on the lam was sure to have murdered his wife for insurance money because people with big bucks always want more. Turned out the doc was framed, but still, ever see that *Oliver* movie about every greedy orphan wanting, more, more, more gruel?"

Hmmm.

"On the other hand, while the *Double Indemnity* case as written up by James Cain was a can of corn—ordinary murder for insurance money—Raymond Chandler had a hand in the documentary film, and you know what that means, Mr. Maximo."

"Remind me."

"Can or worms. Just like Chandler delved into the sordid circumstances surrounding what looked like a simple case of blackmail in *Case of The Big Sleep*, in the documentary film version of *Case of Double Indemnity* he reported not only the obvious

love triangle angle involving the *femme fatale*, her husband and the insurance salesman, but three other three-sided set-ups with potential for murrrderrr."

Max began to have second thoughts about second chances as the smarty-pants kid went on to point out that the *femme fatale* in *Case of Double Indemnity*, a broad named Phyllis Somebody, had been a nurse; suspected by a stepdaughter of killing her husband's first wife.

"Yeah, so what?"

"And the stepdaughter, Lola, came onto the insurance salesman, Walter, who fell for her like a sack of turnips off a farm truck, which was why he turned on the *femme fatale*."

"Again, so what?"

"In my book—or rather in Chandler's documentary film—the sleaziest actor of the bunch was the stepdaughter's boyfriend, Nino, who got involved in a fourth triangle with the *femme fatale* and joined her plot to kill the insurance salesman, Walter, who knew too much."

"Listen-and-learn, kid. The *femme fatale* got what was coming to her in the end. Case closed."

"Yeah, right; Walter offed her after she shot him, to protect the stepdaughter, Lola."

Hmmm.

"I'm just saying, Mr. Maximo, the film version of *Case of Double Indemnity* is considered by many to be the most intriguing in *Noir* history, which means James Cain's written report would have been one of the biggest bestsellers in history if he had dug deeper into the can."

Hmmm.

"And by the way, Boss, according to my cousin who works weekends at the country club, a snooty Mrs. Everheart who hangs there is no big-boobed bimbo; she's flat-chested and must be almost fifty."

Max had to admit, silently to himself, that his lay—now re-named *Case of the Baron and the Old Bimbo*—might turn out to be wormy as a fisherman's bait can. But again, at least he

knew where his next meal would be coming from. And as some wiseguy had scrawled on the wall of the Wide-O-Wake Cafe men's room: good things came from cans, not can'ts.

CHAPTER FOUR

Mamie Motley looked out a kitchen window to a large backyard where her almost thirty-year-old son, Algernon, tended to a gaggle of grounded ducks. Her feelings were mixed. She was happy to have Algie home after being overseas for almost ten years. She was gratified that he was trying, with signs of success, to live vestiges of a dream salvaged from a nightmare. But she worried.

Was it her son's dream to own and operate a restaurant in his small Oklahoma hometown, or was the venture born of stubborn desire to redeem his father's dream?

Was Algie truly driven, as he claimed, to do both well and good, or was his ambition to avenge the hurtful treatment previously suffered by both father and son at the hands of local yokels?

Tall, gangly and stooped even as a teenager, her son had first been cruelly dubbed "Icabod" by junior high schoolmates, no doubt after the nerdy character portrayed in *The Legend of Sleepy Hollow*. Then, perhaps due to his longish pointed nose and admittedly somewhat funereal personality, peers had more meanly taken to calling him "The Buzzard". And finally, the cruelest cut of all, started not by kids but by the stepmother of a girl in his high school class...

Mamie shuddered to recall her own youthful mistake, consequences of which had been visited upon her only child.

As the daughter of an ambitious "stage mother" of sorts, she had been a beauty pageant queen beginning at age six. As such, admittedly, she had basked in the glory, not knowing and/or not

caring about the envy instilled by small town celebrity. Upon being named a *Kraft Cheese* American debutante at age nineteen, she had lobbied the also ambitious mother of her best friend, Mimi Goodrich, to pay for the honor of being also presented to society at a "Camelot Ball" in London, England.

Both mothers were of the Grace Kelly generation. Both had aspirations that their daughters too would bed, if not a Prince of Monaco, a European aristocrat of lofty rank and title. But…

Mamie sighed. She had never been abroad. She did not speak French. She mistook *garcon* to mean "soldier". In a London Court Hotel stairwell following her presentation at the ball, she thought the young man who had also ducked out for a cigarette… Well, in her defense, Larry Jamieson had been wearing a uniform that, except for absence of medals, was not unlike the also red-coated one worn by Prince Andrew, to whom she had curtsied. In a British accent, he said he was enrolled at a Cordon Bleu Institute, and would soon be joining an Escoffier Brigade. One thing led to another and…

Again Mamie sighed. Her easily seduced "soldier" had done the honorable thing. Upon being told of her "delicate" condition—perhaps also laboring under the mistaken assumption that her parents were wealthy—he had crossed an ocean to be at her side a few days after Algie's birth. With her father's financial backing, they had opened a restaurant called *Maison des Crepes*. Working hand-in-hand to the bone, they had been too busy and/or too tired to officially tie a marital knot, which was just as well, seeing as how it turned out that Larry was already married to a woman back in England.

The restaurant failed of course. With tail between his legs, the father of her toddling son returned to London. And years later—following a high school prom—Mimi Goodrich Everheart had screeched insults about Algernon "The Bastard" Motley, who had leapt onto a stage and bit off the head of a live pigeon—which was not all that unusual behavior for local boys his age—but then smacked a bloody kiss on the lips of a prom queen.

Mamie sighed yet again. As a single mother working full-time as a nurse, she had done her best to raise her unusual boy under often trying circumstances.

As an infant, Algie had responded to cooing. He had babbled as normal. As a toddler, he had played imaginatively, though awkwardly. He was not particularly anxious nor difficult to console. But doctors said Algie was born at the low end of a so-called Autism Spectrum Disorder. And as he grew older, he had become maddeningly prone to physical tics and outbursts of "verbal self stimulation"—sometimes called stereotypy or simming—displaying way too loud, almost always inappropriate repetitive recitation of learned words and phrases, mainly from nursery rhymes that even now remained stuck inside his head.

"Goosey goosey gander/ Where shall I wander?" he would yell over and over again as he obsessively attended to whatever had caught his interest. "Pease porridge hot, pease porridge cold/ Pease porridge in the pot, nine days old/ Some like it hot, some like it cold/ Some like it in the pot, nine days old." And so on, and on, and on at the top of his voice. Sometimes she thought he might have been putting on an act of being "eccentric" in order to either draw or divert attention to or away from himself.

After graduating from high school her socially misfit son felt he had to get out of what he rightly called "this Godforsaken place" where "nobody likes me, everybody hates me/ I think I'll go eat worms," he had hollered, relatively cheerfully. "I'll bite off their heads, and suck the juice/ and throw the skins away/ Down goes the first one, down goes the second one/ Oh how they wiggle and squirm", etcetera, etcetera, etcetera.

And under the circumstances—though he had never said and she had never asked—she had supposed it was only natural for an eighteen-year-old boy to seek out the father he had never known. Whether or not they ever made a connection, she supposed it was also only natural for him to follow in his father's footsteps at the Cordon Bleu cooking school in London.

But again, was it natural for Algie to then return to what he now called "this Godblessed Garden of Eden", and take up where his father had left off?

He'd had an "epiphany", her son said, brought on by a magazine article, titled *Guts and Grease: The Diet of Native Americans,* about the ongoing research of a Weston A. Price Foundation dedicated to restoring "Wise Traditions in Food, Farming, and Healing Arts". Contrary to "politically correct" notions that the originally remarkable health and fitness of native peoples was attributable to diets rich in polyunsaturated fatty acids but very low in saturated fat, the foundation's namesake founder had found that just the opposite had been the case. Studies showed that Plains Indians and Eskimos had thrived on consumption of a wide variety of saturated fat sources ranging from bear grease to buffalo guts.

Upon his return to Oklahoma, Algie had thrown back his head of long black hair, flapped his elbows as he'd habitually done since childhood, ♫My heart knows what the wild goose knows ♫ he had semi-sung. ♫Wild goose, brother goose, which is best?/ A wanderin' fool or a heart at rest?/ Wild gooooose… ♫

Somewhat more sensibly, "Behold the wise ways of the wild geese. The wild goose and gander store fat for the arduous task of migration, and thereby set an example for us all."

Still gazing out the kitchen window as her son tended to chores, Mamie's mood changed to unmitigated maternal glow. With combined savings they had bought a building on the west edge of town that had once been the premises of a large restaurant called *Chair Crushers,* featuring an all-you-can-eat buffet. Algie had arranged for services of a "motley" group of young men and women—he called them "wranglers"—to forage throughout the county and beyond for wild and stray animals.

She handled the paperwork, seldom venturing through the skinning-and-butchering room after witnessing…Well, while she had come to accept the notion that means of butchering meat did not necessarily make roadkill inedible, she had never seen a skinned fox, and was appalled by sight of a catlike carcass.

Now supposedly brilliant chefs at first-rate restaurants in the big cities of America were catching on to lost wisdom of both aboriginal peoples and wild geese, to the point that…

Mamie looked down at a mail-out flyer lying on a kitchen counter, headed **PRAIRIE HOME MEATS, Henryetta, Oklahoma,** *Chef Algernon Motley, Proprietor…*

listing **INDIAN CORN-FED DUCK/** *Chef's Choice…* **PRIVATE RESERVE PORK/** *Stye Curated* **…LAZY C RANCH LAMB/** *Poacher's Pride…*

and **NATIVE AMERICAN FREE-RANGE GAME**

including **Baby Buffalo Ribs…Rack of Raccoon…Possum Potpourri…Wild Turkey Legs…Okmulgee County Squab-n-Squirrel Combo…Cool-Air Cured Coyote…**

AND MUCH MORE!

Algie worked day-and-night to keep up with orders that poured in from fancy big city restaurants, and slept in a back room. The business operated at maximum capacity, but… There was of course a catch. Though a one-pound squirrel could be "wrangled" at a unit cost of, say, one dollar, and sold for ten dollars, net profits were marginal, at best. Algie saw the problem as inefficiency and waste. From a bookkeeping point of view she had to agree.

Still, she had been dubious of his proposed solution. She had strenuously argued against the notion that local rednecks would appreciate—and pay for—Algie's sophisticated cuisine, but… "I'll cram it down their throats," he'd said, with a wild look in his dark eyes, "and make them like it!"

With her son beside her, Mamie was now re-living a chapter of her past life. He had somehow acquired an industrial-strength meat grinder. She had retrieved her deceased mother's set of *Everlasting Leadware.* Foraging at estate sales, they found more of the branded skillets, pots and pans once marketed with a slogan of "Guaranteed to Outlive You". Uncrushed chairs and tables were already on hand. And this time, with she in "the counting house" keeping the books, and Algie in an adjacent kitchen, back to repetitively rapping so-called "songs" from his childhood…

Mamie picked up another sheet of paper from the counter:
PRAIRIE HOME CAFE
Henryetta, Oklahoma
MENU
BLEEDING HEARTS BURGER..... $10
CHICKEN FRIED BRAINS..... $8
WAGGING TONGUE BURGER..... $10
TABLE SCRAPS PATTY..... $5
LIVERING LARGE BURGER..... $10
FAVA BEAN SALAD..... $3
PRAIRIE OYSTER BURGER..... $10
KID'S KIDNEY NUGGETS..... $3
BIG CHARCOLON BURGER..... $10
SWEETBREAD PUDDING..... $4
MYSTERY PIE OF THE DAY..... $5
Everything slathered with Chef Algie's Secret Sauce*

Contrary to her expectation, since the cafe's opening more than a month ago local yokels had been lining up to gobble up ground up animal parts—called offal—that had mostly gone to waste before. And the profits, well, at $5-a-pop the Table Scraps Patty, called scrapple in the eastern U.S. and consisting mostly of ground up pig parts—snout-to-tail or "everything but the oink"—was <u>all</u> profit.

It was Algie's so-called Secret Sauce that turned sows ears into silk purses. Whereas hearts, tongues, livers and other organs of cattle, sheep, and poultry were nothing new in other regions…

Mamie's mood suddenly darkened. Instinctively, like a farmer's wife who had spotted a rodent, she picked up a kitchen knife and rushed out the door. In the backyard, now sidled up next to her unsuspecting son was none other than Mimi Goodrich's overweight stepdaughter, Sugar Everheart. It was that not so little rat, as a teenager, who had spread her cruel stepmother's nickname for Algie and ruined…

"Sugar's going to be staying here for awhile…"

"Thanks so much for taking me in, Mrs. Motley."

"…and help me make Secret Sauce."

At sight of the unattractive young woman grabbing hold of a duck by its neck and prying open its mouth for Algie to pour a can of corn down its gullet, Mamie, in a near rage, felt utterly sick to her stomach. In his literal way of seeing things, her naive son seemed inclined to forgive-and-forget being called illegitimate. But not Mamie. Oh no, she, The Bastard's illegitimate mother, would never forget, and would damned sure never forgive!

CHAPTER FIVE

As usual, Max had a date with his mom to watch private detective documentaries on TV. And tonight's lay would be no after-dinner piece of cake. A fellow P.I.—Joe Mannix—had been left in a tight spot at the end of a Part I of a DVD record of a two-part 1975 *Case of a Bird of Prey*. And Joe had already took twenty squirts of lead plus at least fifty brutal beatings during his seven-year gumshoe career.

Also, as Mom and he re-worked the case, he would have to put aside nagging worry about his own current client—O.B. Everheart—and focus on the question of...

Who wants to be Queen for a Day?

RAHHHHHHH...

"Let's watch this MeTV oldie tonight, Maxie," said Mom from beside him on a love seat. "Jack Bailey is so handsome, and...Well, I'm in the mood for a Cinderella Story."

Do you want to be Queen for a Day?!

YESSSSSSS...

Though they had previously seen possibly this same episode of the repetitive re-runs of the game show, Max shoveled another handful of hot buttered popcorn into his pie hole and pretended to be interested.

From a large studio audience of all broads, four queen candidates would be picked at random. Each would be interviewed by Bailey—a smooth operator with black mustache and slicked-back hair—who would crack funny jokes to take the edge off the sob stories told by the wannabe queens. Audience choice of the one most pathetically worthy of royal honor would

be determined by a meter that measured applause. All the others would remain lifetime losers.

But the programs mostly consisted of fashion shows and commercials that advertised women's clothes and household goods wanted and needed by broads. And the nagging thoughts… Well, thanks to the nit-picking kid, his current *Case of the Baron and the Old Bimbo* now looked not so much like Percy Wilson's *Case of Mister Big Bucks and Miss Big Boobs*-- in which the *femme* was a dumb blonde and not all that *fatale*—as possibly more like the not so simple *Case of Double Indemnity.*

Wait, don't tell me, Wanda. I'll bet I can guess what you want for your unlucky little boy. Brain surgery, right?

No, if I get to be queen I would like to have a screen test and become a glamorous movie star.

RAHHHHHHH…

And now, here's a word you don't want to miss from Sani-Flush. Ladies, is your husband a big eater?

On the other hand, the green-as-grass kid was inclined to make ham salad out of circumstances simple as sliced ham sandwiches. Though O.B. Everheart's double-dealing spouse was an older sort of bimbo, and possibly not a blonde, chances were she and her side man were too dumb to make her hubby disappear before Yours Truly got the goods on them

Speaking of toupees, Thelma, what is it called when a king and queen have no children?

Quiet in the house?

No, receding "heir" line. Ha, ha, ha. Get it? H-e-i-r. Ha, ha, ha…

Mine has receded all the way down to my ears; and …Please, Mr. Bailey, I need another Kleenex to wipe off tears.

Ha, ha, ha. Baldness will teach you not to light matches next time you to check your motorcycle gas tank. Ha, ha, ha…

Or it could be that the client's brain had, uh, receded. The old codger may have forgot to mention all the poop-and-circumstances bearing on the danger he was in.

And now this word from Odor Eater shoe inserts. Ladies, does your husband come to bed with…?

"Sorry, Mom," said Max, rising from the love seat. "Gotta run downtown and check a few details my client may have overlooked."

"Shush! I want to hear what this poor one-legged woman has to say about why she deserves to be Queen for a Day."

Max heeled-and-toed through the kitchen and out the back door. At the wheel of his mom's brown Buick boiler, he put pedal to the metal. Driving toward downtown, flotsam of sorts began to wash up on the edges of his mind:

O.B. Everheart's first Missus was named "Honeybee"… Now a *femme fatale* whose name was pronounced "MeMe" was the queen bee… Having mated with her—according to a high school Biology Class teacher—the hubby would have been expected to drop dead, but…Though more of a checkers player than chess man, he knew how the pieces moved. Queens ran around yelling, "Off with their heads!" …At that very moment, a "Queen's Jubilee" was about to take place overseas, despite—or maybe because—Her Majesty's mate, a joker named Prince Phillip, had recently dropped dead. Hmmm.

With all that buzzing inside his head, Max put on the brakes out front of the Fountainblue Motel, got out of the boiler, and hotfooted past the joint's check-in window into an open-air courtyard surrounded by numbered guest rooms. At the door marked ♪8…Uh oh, from inside the client's room came the sound of voices.

After checking that his Roscoe was holstered inside his jacket, he tried the knob and…For crying out loud, O.B. Everheart had ignored or forgotten his instructions and left the door unlocked. He pushed it slightly open and…

Eighty muu muus? What the heck, Lillian, I see that you yourself could use two of the loose dresses, but eighty? Ha, ha, ha.

Like I said, unfortunate girls at the Oklahoma City prep school have always wanted to eat a whole pig at a real luau, and me too.

Max busted into the room and saw that O.B. Everheart was propped up in bed and also watching…

"Hold your horses, podner," said the client. "Dang it, if it was up to me I'd see to it that every one of those underprivileged gals got to be Queen for a Day."

Having no interest in manly underwear called *Depends*, Max ignored another commercial that appeared on the TV screen and got down to business.

"Just a couple of details, Mr. Everheart. You said you met your second wife at a lonely hearts square dance after the first one bought the farm, right?"

"Not exactly. Before we met doing an allemande-left, Mimi was what they call a Junior League volunteer at the hospital, but a downright Big League angel in my book. Knowin' that Honeybee had a sweet tooth, Mimi sneaked in cakes, cookies and candy to make her happy. We didn't do-si-do 'til after..."

Who wants Wanda to be Queen for a Day?
RAHHH...

"And about that only child you and the first Missus hatched, how do she and her stepmother get along?"

"Well, only so-so, now that you mention it."

Who wants Thelma to be Queen for a Day?
RAHHHHHHH...

"See, Mr. Morgan, Sugar has took up with a boyfriend—a fancy chuck wagon hand named Algernon Motley—and for some reason Mimi doesn't cotton to the young man."

Who wants Annie Mae to be Queen for a Day?
RAHHHHHHHHHH...

"Just one more question, Mr. Everheart. Being a cattle baron, I don't suppose you would see any need for insurance to make sure Mimi is happy after you disappear, would you?"

Who wants Lillian be Queen for a Day?
RAHHHHHHHHHHHHHHHH...

"Between you and me, podner," said the client in a lowered voice, "I have just about gone bust tryin' to make Mimi happy. Debts up to my ears. So at her suggestion I recently went to see her friend, young Bailey.'"

"Jack Bailey, the guy who crowns Queens for a Day?"

"No, ol' Buford Bailey, who eats at the Dairy Queen."

"<u>Mayor</u> Buford Bailey?"

"Well yeah, Buford and his daddy before him have handled public affairs along with insurance here in town since Gus was a pup. Him and Mimi went to high school at about the same time and have since become chummy."

"Big-butt Buford Bailey?!"

"I know, he's a RINO, but I am semi-hopeful that when I… when I disappear, Buford will see to it that Mimi is took care of."

So Ladies, if the spark has gone out of your own Cinderella Story, use a dab of Mother Finegan's all-purpose starch to set things straight between you and your Prince Charming.

After Jack Bailey had promised to have an outlet of Robertson's Hams in the nearby town of Seminole deliver eighty-one smoked pigs to an Oklahoma City prep school, that graduation song about pomp-and-circumstances began to play. As the funny TV show host then put a crown on the head of a new Queen for a Day, Max decided that under the circumstances—with a *femme fatale*, an insurance salesman, a daughter and sleazy boyfriend in the mix—he'd better bunk there at the motel with the client.

In other words, yeah, like the vegetarian fall guy found out the hard way in Percy Wilson's *Case of Two Pigs and Sweet Potatoes in a Blanket*, interlocking love triangles made for strange bedfellows.

TUESDAY

June 3, 2022

CHAPTER SIX

With Princess Di's smudged wine glass in hand, Mimi again paced the floor of her mansion's Hall of Heraldry. After sleeping, or rather not sleeping on how to handle the British Crown's Chancery of Justice bully sent to deliver a warrant for her arrest, she had decided not to lie, but to simply suggest a more likely alternative possibility for how the treasured Princess Diana artifact had come into her possession, to-wit:

Yes, someone must have climbed over the locked gate at Diana's ancestral home. Someone must have entered the otherwise closed Althorp House gift shoppe and discovered the poignant memorial to the beloved saint's last supper at the Ritz Hotel in Paris… A table set for two…A half-eaten hunk of cheese…A few crumbs of bread…And the wine glass, smudged with the princess' lipstick, that had been removed from not-for-sale display at Harrods. At perhaps the sound of a toilet flushing, that someone must have impulsively seized the precious memento and fled the touching scene.

She would explain that through the years of her marriage to a typical low-born but jumped-up rich American rancher, her crass husband had tastelessly attempted to attain high-class status through acquisition of such objects. He was forever paying for impedimenta of nobility advertised online and in magazines. The Hall's display of coats-of-arms representing family names found in her ancestry, for instance, were all bought and paid for by her spouse to reflect glory on himself by association.

Likely fearful of today's reckoning for theft of the priceless relic that had once touched the lips of Princess Diana, her

cowardly husband had fled to his detestable cattle ranch. She herself on the other hand, suspecting dodgy provenance of the no doubt "fenced" wine glass—not to mention likely presence of Camilla's fingerprints—had notified the F.B.I. months ago in hope and expectation the evidence would…

"A major, a batman, and an aide-de-camp are here to see you, Mrs. Everheart," a housemaid announced.

Mimi bounded to a tall, distinguished, somehow familiar-looking man attired in a British military red coat bedecked with medals, and extended the ill-gotten wine glass to him. "At last, Major! I have long awaited this opportunity to honor the saintly woman the world has long adored."

"Well, bit early in the day for me, but… What say you, Bates?" he said, doffing his sporty pith helmet and looking toward the less tall, less distinguished-looking yellow-haired man in camouflage apparel and red beret who stood at attention beside him.

"'Air of the dog never 'urts, Major," said the man, "Bates", with a glance toward antique crystal decanters of liquor set on a side table.

"Will you let your 'air down a bit and join us, Vickers?" said the major to a youngish, stern-faced woman also beside him, who silently turned and went to the side table.

"Major Lawrence Jesterson, O.B.E. with Grape Leaf Cluster, Retired; at your service, Madam," said the Crown Chancery's big-game bounty hunter, with a click of his booted heels. "And may I say, how fitting for this occasion are these surroundings and your personal trappings."

"I always dress modestly, Major," said Mimi, having chosen a black, floor-length nun-like habit for the dreaded encounter. "In homage to…"

"Yes, quite so," he replied, raising the now whiskey-filled wine glass and gazing toward an enlarged newspaper photo stuck onto the wall in place of Diana's portrait. "God save the Queen!"

"Ere 'Ere."

"Is that the Duchess of Cornwall in the background?" the youngish woman asked, moving closer to the photo. "I have

never known the future queen to wear black-framed spectacles and…My word, is Camilla now missing a <u>front</u> tooth?"

"A recent fall from a horse perhaps," Mimi ventured, and to further explain the Hall decor: "I am a loyal Daughter of King George III and rue the day this colony sided with that upstart, George Washington. Except for the Botsford Family plaque, however, all of the Hall's, store-bought, uh, effects are my husband's choices of decor, for which I bear no…"

"'Usband?!" said the major, swatting his thigh with a swagger stick. "Did I not make myself crystal on the dog yesterday, Madam?"

"On the dog?"

"Dog-and-bone, Ma'am," said the "batman", Bates. "Means phone in Olde Blighty."

"As the Baked Bean's ears-and-eyes, I cannot acknowledge sound-or-sight of any spouse or offspring until pending matters are properly settled."

"Baked Bean?"

"Means Queen, Ma'am."

"My…the man claiming to be my husband has, uh, disappeared as you instructed, Major. Have mercy."

Seemingly satisfied, and with the wine glass refilled by his batman, Major Jesterson sat down at head of the Hall's long table. His aide-de-camp, Vickers, took a rolled-up parchment from an attache case and handed it to him. He unrolled the document, put on reading glasses, and… oh no, here it came. Expecting to hear a recital of formal charges…

"Ah yes, 'ere is told the ancient tale of Good King 'Enry's visitation onto the Estate of the Right 'Honourable Barnum FitzBailey, Baron of Bridgewater, during which 'is Late Majesty picked the Baron's youngest daughter, Cecilia, to warm the cockles of his bed following an Eve of Feast and Frolic.

"For the benefit of those unversed in Olde Blighty's medieval 'istory, I shall read the entirety of the record aloud:

"'This mayden bright cecilie, as 'ir lif seith/ Was comen of romayns, and of noble kynde/ And from 'ir craydel up fostred

in the feith/ O crist, and bar 'is gospel in 'ir mynde/ She nevere cessed, as I written fynde/ Of 'ir preyere, and God to love and drede/ Bisekynge 'ym to kepe 'ir maydenhede.

"'And whan this mayden in 'ir bede did fynde/ A king wythe not marriage on 'is mynde/ To God allone in 'erte thus sang she/ O lord, my soule and and eek my body gye/ Unwemmed, lest that it confounded be/ And, for 'is love that dyde upon a tree.

"'Fie upon thee, cryde 'e, eternal barreness thee shall bee/ If thou dost marry, I give this plague for thy dowry/ Be thou as chaste as ice, as pur as sno/ Get thee to a nunnery, go!'"

Mimi was entirely bewildered by the recitation of Olde Blighty history, but…The major took off the reading specs, looked up from the parchment, and continued:

"In less olde English, 'istory tells us that the Baron, as directed by the King, dedicated a goodly portion of 'is estate to an Order of nuns in the name of and to be governed by his youngest daughter, Virgin Cecilia. In centuries that followed, the Order spread to other convents, each and all in'erited by Cecilia's youngest daughter's youngest daughter's youngest daughter, etcetera, etcetera, etcetera."

Mimi was more confused, but…

Major Jesterson again drained the smudged wine glass, then went on to explain: Yes, Cecelia and succeeding youngest daughters gave birth to succeeding youngest daughters. They were often virgins in name only prior their respective investitures, and always virgins in title only after open display of motherhood. Maintenance of appearances in the eyes of the Sovereign was the protocol that mattered. And eventually, it appeared that Cecilia's line of daughters died out.

Weary of the longwinded preamble, "Your glass, Major; notice that it bears evidence of…"

"Evidence of being empty, says I. 'Ave another, Sir?"

"Well, just a drop, Bates. Sun must be over a yardarm somewhere, what?"

"It's evidence I reported to the F.B.I. Camilla's fingerprints may well…"

"Now where was I? Ah yes, some years ago our good Queen Elizabeth, besieged with titular claims, established by Royal Warrant a Lost & Found Department within the Crown Chancery, trusted keeper of the Roll of Peerage. All thousands of such claims inspired by online and magazine adverts proved to be bogus results of scams perpetrated upon America's social climbing 'oi polloi. Needless to say, the Bean was not amused. As a result of redoubled efforts under my command, 'owever, I am pleased to announce that you, Madam Botsford…"

"My, uh, unmarried maydenhede name is actually Goodrich."

"Pleased, I say, to announce that you, Madam Goodrich, 'ave been found to be the current youngest daughter of—etcetera, etcetera, etcetera— the Virgin Cecelia of Bridgewater Abbey. Congratulations."

Thrilled to have, at last, an actual connection to a family of noble standing, Mimi imagined a FitzBailey family crest, if not also a portrait of herself, prominently displayed on the wall currently devoted exclusively to Princess Diana. The Legacy Arts Company's once-in-a-lifetime 50% Off Sale of 24-carat gilded plaques would likely have expired by now, but O.B. would no doubt welcome extra expenditure to make her last days happy.

"In addition, the Lost & Found Department 'as determined that this fellow, Chauncey, who scribed…"

"Beg pardon, Major, I believe the name is Chaucer. Geoffrey Chaucer."

"Yes, quite. Thank you, Vickers. Now, where was I? Ah yes, my department has found that this Chaucer fellow, the civil servant who scribed the Virgin Cecilia's 'istory, mis-scribed Good King 'Enry's pronouncement of 'barreness'. Context, including Lady Cecilia's birthing of a bastard child nine months after her rather overwrought vow of chastity, clearly shows dowry granted by 'Is late Majesty to Cecelia and her youngest daughter's youngest daughter's etcetera was the 'ereditary title of 'Baroness'. Therefore, by Royal Warrant, it is my duty to inform you…"

"I myself am Baroness of Bridgewater?!"

"'Heiress <u>presumptive</u> to the title of Virgin Baroness of Bridgewater <u>Abbey</u>, Madam. Until rites of investiture 'ave been properly conducted…'"

Alas, there was always a catch, Mimi rued, as the major commenced to drone on about the Bean's aged feeble condition…the possibility of Her Majesty's imminent demise or abdication…the possibility that King Charles and Queen Camilla, damn them, might revoke the Royal Warrant…the likelihood that other claimants to the title would come out of woodwork…etcetera, etcetera, etcetera…but then…

"Just spit-balling, Major," said Ms. Vickers. "Might not investiture of the Virgin Baroness Mimi be conducted here and now?"

"'Ere? In the colonies? Now? Without time for proper…?"

"Her Majesty's Platinum Jubilee kicks off on Thursday, Major. What better way to honor Her Royal Highness than to celebrate the joyous occasion with pomp-and-ceremony far-and-wide?"

"By Jove, Vickers, why not?!" said the Crown's official representative, with a slap of his swagger stick to the table. "Time is indeed short, but I myself could put the presumptive Virgin Baroness through the paces preparatory to formal rites. You, Vickers, could arrange for a fitting Feast of Investiture. Bates shall stand ready to provide transport, 'eavy lifting, and…I say, Madam, what say you?"

Mimi lunged forward, seized the half-full wine glass, raised the vessel from which Diana had last imbibed, and bellowed: "I say, God save the Virgin Baroness of Bridgewater Abbey!"

"Bully!"

"Capital!"

"'Ere 'Ere!"

CHAPTER SEVEN

Max only semi-hotfooted down a Main Street sidewalk, thanks to having rolled out of a sagging bed at the Fountainblue Hotel with a crick in his back. The so-called queen-size bunk was too small for two jumbo-size guys such as O. B. Everheart and himself. And the motel provided a limited amount of hot water for soaking in an also undersized tub. Which was just as well as things turned out. Otherwise it might not have occurred to him to take the endangered client home — with a pillowcase over his head — for breakfast and a shower.

With Mom keeping an eye on him, the targeted husband would be safer than at the Fountainblue, where yesterday the motel proprietor — a baldheaded oddball named Lice — had talked the old codger into playing checkers at a table set up in the joint's open-air courtyard. Both were dumb-lucky not to have been knocked off like ducks in a barrel by Buford Bailey.

Yeah, the kid had made a lucky guess: *Case of the Baron and the Old Bimbo* was in fact a dead ringer for *Case of Double Indemnity* involving a related life ensurance scam. And yeah, the situation looked to possibly involve multiple love triangles. But so what? The two-against-one set-up in play that threatened his client was the one pairing the old rancher's second wife — an obvious *femme fatale* who likely killed the first wife with a sugar overdose — and Bailey. The town's Mayor, otherwise an unlikely would-be accomplice to murrrderrr, had the bad luck to also be an insurance salesman.

Unfortunately for the bim and her side man, however, Yours Truly had long ago mastered the *Double Indemnity's* documentary case report, line-for-line.

Chances were that Bailey had been knocking door-to-door; got a foot inside the *femme fatale's* big house and half-wittingly put a price on her hubby's head by pitching a life insurance deal. Chances were the deadly dame had batted her baby blues and said something along the lines of, say: "I was just fixing some ice tea. Would you like a glass?"

Chances were Bailey took the bait and cracked wise along the lines of, say: "Sure, unless you've got a bottle of beer that's also out of order."

Yeah, it was the same old story going back to the one about a Garden of Eatin'. His job was to write a happy ending.

Arrived at the storefront entrance to Bailey's business bailiwick, Max paused to catch his breath. With a pat of hand, he checked that Old Junior Jr. was holstered and ready to… Okay, the plastic replica of Mike Hammer's .45 gat only squirted liquids, but had a dangerous look to it that made most mopes think twice about making a false move.

Inside the office, he was met by a youngish dame sitting at a desk, filing her fingernails and chewing gum at the same time.

"Looking to have a little chat with a certain insurance salesman who makes a habit of knocking on doors of old bimbos."

"Mr. Buford is not in at the moment. He's delivering some print materials to…"

"Let me guess. The boss is going ever the fine print of a double indemnity insurance policy at the residence of Mrs. Mimi Everheart, right?"

"He didn't say and I am not at liberty to repeat it."

"But you happened to overhear him talking on the blower, didn't you, Dollface," said Max said, reaching into a jacket pocket and…

"That would be eavesdropping, which I am not at liberty to…."

…then waving a light green refresher in the skirt's face.

"Dollar-to-a-donut, you heard the boss man say something along the lines of, say: "Watch your step, Baby, every single minute. Straight down the line.' Right?"

"Well, yes, Mr. Buford may have said something along those lines, but not to Mrs. Everheart. He was talking to a Mrs. Morgan, who lives on East Willow Street."

Mrs. Morgan on East Willow Street?!

Max bolted from the office, hotfooted full-bore up Main Street; jumped into the parked brown boiler and put pedal to the metal.

His mom — though well aware he was fair-skinned and susceptible to sun poisoning — had nevertheless recently took to talking about selling their house and moving to Florida, the Sunshine State! He had written off the chatter as typical female fantasy, provoked by a past episode of *Queen for a Day* in which a good-looking blonde from Kalamora, Michigan won a bus ticket to a swinging old folks hot spot called Boca Grande. Though it was hard to believe his own mother would even contemplate buying an insurance policy on him and committing...

Max brought the boiler to a screeching halt in the driveway of the East Willow Street house that had been his home since birth, jumped out of the vehicle and hotfooted toward the back door, but...

Inside the kitchen, it hit him like a burping-slap to his backside: Mom was at the table, playing checkers and eating ice cream with... In a passing moment of unfounded panic, he had forgot bringing O.B. Everheart home earlier. Obviously, Buford Bailey had tailed them from the motel but...

"Yes, the Mayor came by with re-election brochures," said his mom. "He wanted to put campaign signs in the front yard, but I told him we would not be supporting a RINO."

"Ol' Buford should stick to sellin' insurance and quit botherin' pretty gals, if you ask me," said O.B. Everheart. "Your move, 'Queenie'."

Hmmm. Bailey had probably backed off a move against the old codger after spotting a witness on the premises, Max thought, as he ankled out the door.

But may have taken the opportunity to case the joint for a later move, he thought, as he got back into the boiler.

Or the would-be perp might have got cold feet, Max speculated, as he again put pedal to the metal.

In any case, the dame dizzy rhino would likely have headed back to the *femme fatale,* to make or face the music. Speaking of which…

♫*I went down to the sacred store/ Where I'd heard the music years before…* ♫

Maybe because he was feeling peckish, an old song had begun to play inside his bean.

♫*So, bye-bye, Miss American Pie/ Drove my Chevy to the levee, but the levee was dry/ And them good ol' boys were drinkin' whiskey and rye/ Singin'…* ♫

Fifteen minutes later, arrived at the entrance to a long driveway leading to the Everheart mansion…Hel-lo, a black stretch-limo—with little flags on sticks stuck to its hood—came barreling between two stone pillars onto the road and headed west.

Max gave chase.

♫*Bye-bye, Miss American Pie…* ♫

Dark tinted windows of the limo made it impossible to see who was inside, which meant he was tailing blind.

♫*I was a lonely teenaged bronkin' buck/ But I knew I was out of luck…* ♫

Though unable to make out the handprinted details, he could see that the limo sported a temporary cardboard tag, meaning it had been recently acquired.

♫*Now for ten years we've been on our own/ And moss grows fat on a rollin' stone…* ♫

By getting onto an Interstate 40 service road, the vehicle appeared to be headed toward Oklahoma City.

♫*So, bye-bye, Miss American Pie/ Drove my Chevy to the levee, but…* ♫

Instead, the limo pulled into the parking lot of a joint—identified by a large sign as PRAIRIE HOME CAFE—that looked to now occupy the building where the Chair Crushers Buffet used to serve all-you-can-eat chow.

As his stomach began to growl, the limo's passenger-side front door came open. Out stepped a dame, wearing a khaki jacket and matching skirt, with a briefcase in hand. At a hurried pace, she ankled into the cafe.

Out of the boiler, heel-and-toeing after her, Max noticed a chrome medallion—*Dean Motor Company, Oklahoma City, OK*—stuck onto the parked limo's somewhat faded and slightly dented rear-end door. Faintly visible on a back-seat window were traces of previously glued-on decal for *Sunny Lane Funeral Home.*

Inside the cafe, the dame with the briefcase looked to have already put in an order at a stand-up counter before moving to a single chair set beside a door signed *Management Office.*

Max took off his fedora, ankled up to the counter, and eyeballed a wall-mounted menu board. From behind the counter…

"Welcome to the Prairie Home Cafe," said a young dame, suspiciously named "Sugar" according to a label stuck to her shirt. "Today's mid-morning Burger-of-the-Day is…"

"Just a slice of the 'Mystery Pie', Sweetheart, with cheese on top for sweeteners."

"Sorry, no cheese and no slices. We serve only whole Mystery Meat Pies, sweetened with Chef Algie's Secret Sauce."

Only whole pies? Hmmm. Whether or not his tail of the dame proved to be a wild goose chase, Max had a hunch that he—like Little Jack Horner, so to speak—had stuck in a thumb and got lucky.

♫ *So, bye-bye, Miss American Pie…* ♫

CHAPTER EIGHT

"'Cause I'm Slim Shady/ Yes, I'm the real Shady/ He could be working at Burger King/ spittin' on your onion rings…'"

With her son loudly rapping in the adjacent Prairie Home Foods & Cafe kitchen, "No, we would <u>not</u> be able to manage a Thursday feast for seventy couples," said Mamie, rising from her desk inside the company management office.

"'Yeah, I probably got a few screws up in my head loose/ But it's cool for Tom Green to hump a dead moose…'"

"And before you ask, Ms. Vickers, the answer to your possibly next inquiry is also <u>no</u>. If we did have 'Prince Albert in a can', we would not let 'him' out , even if the Queen 'called for a pipe and three fiddlers' to celebrate her Platinum Jubilee."

Mamie had no time for the British woman's attempt to stage a way outdated adolescent prank, but as she moved toward the door to show the mossik out…

"I do wish you would extend the colonial courtesy of hearing me out," she said. And just as Algie came through the door: "Cost is no object."

"I'm all ears," said her son, seating himself. "Not literally; just sayin'. Actually, I'm all snips and snails and puppy dog tails, or so they said when I was a lad."

With a sigh, Mamie plopped back into her chair.

In her clipped British accent the starchy Vickers woman again acknowledged the shortness of two days notice for catering the grand affair she had in mind: a traditional "Olde English feast" in celebration of an historic observance.

"Sounds right down my alley," said Algie, before introducing himself and going on to tell that he had lived in London for ten years, where he had been trained in traditional English cuisine dating back to its high water mark, "as exemplified by recipes contained in *The Secretes of Reverende Maister Alexis of Piermont,* circa 1558…"

"That sounds like a French alley."

"…and *Dame Elinor Fettiplace's Receipt Book* compiled in 1604. For instance, 'Take a shoulder of mutton and being halfe roasted, cut it in great slices and save the gravie. Then take Claret wine and…'"

"How serendipitous! Chef Algernon, what would you recommend for the first of, say, ten or twelve courses?"

"Our local oysters, of course. **'O Oysters come and walk with us, the Walrus did beseech/ 'A pleasant walk, a pleasant talk along the sandy…'**"

"Oysters out here on a prairie? How grand! We shall want barrels and barrels of local oysters, all served raw of course."

"As you wish, Ms.…?"

"Vickers, just Vickers will do."

"Next, grilled beaver tails would suit the palette, as well as qualify for the 'fish loophole' convenient for Olde English guests of religious persuasion if the feast goes on into Friday. Slathered with Secret Sauce, beaver tail smells like fish, tastes like chicken."

"Terribly good form!"

"Then spit-roasted wild boar, perhaps quarters of stag would be nice, but…" ♫**A sheep herder came by and built a fence/ I saw him one day but ain't seen him since/ So if you want mutton we got mutton to sell/ Cowpunchers around here are mean as hell**♫

"Yes, by all means. Mutton! Mutton! Mutton!"

"As well as suckling pigs, topped with pounds of whatever animal fat is most readily available."

"Yummy!"

"As for fowl, peacocks dressed with their own iridescent feathers are both traditional and decorative, but locally…No,

wild turkeys are too dull. Hmmm. How about roasted swans accompanied by, say, four singing blackbirds, or pigeons, baked in pies. Wouldn't that be a dainty dish to set before each of your guests!"

"Indeed!"

"I served under Chef Sweeney at the famous Todd's Chop House on Fleet Street in London. Meat pies are my specialty. ♫**Oh where, oh where, has my little dog gone?/ Oh where, oh where...?** ♫

"Speaking of guests," said Mamie. "Seventy couples is a lot of people for a small town such as this. Who...?"

"Yes, that is a bit of a pickle. We shall randomly circulate 'Save the Date' flyers today, but may not have a whittled-down list for suitably engraved invitations until mid-day Thursday."

Mamie began to feel more dubious.

"You'll be wanting plenty of ox parts, of course, tongue-to-tail. And an abundance of *pieds et pacquets*, as well as an assortment of..."

"Nothing French. The major cannot abide the Frogs."

"Yes, of course. I should have said 'trotters', the Olde English term for sheep hooves."

"Much better!"

"As well as an assortment of elder, brawn, sausages and..."

"Old brown sausages? Sounds ghastly."

"Beg your pardon, Ms. Vickers. 'Elder meaning...'"

"Vickers will do."

"'Elder' meaning cow's udder. 'Brawn' meaning head cheese. 'Sausages' meaning pig intestines stuffed with snips, snails, puppy dog tails...."

"I adore head cheese! And we must have hare. I adore baby rabbits."

"No! I am sorry, Vickers, but I must insist," said Algie, rising to his feet and beginning to pace. "As Jack Sprat no doubt found to his regret, those darn wabbits are unfit for human consumption. In times of famine, many a Native American succumbed to what

we call 'rabbit fever', brought on by lean cuisine. Perhaps a few roasted ears and paws, but otherwise…"

"Very well; and no vegetables. A few fava beans perhaps, to go with…I assume you will provide an assortment of rare livers."

"Of course, and gobs of black pudding, only slightly congealed with gelatin." **Georgy Pogy, pudding and pie/ Kissed a girl and made her…"**

"No desserts; just wine. We must have oodles of spirits conducive to merrymaking. Whiskey, wine and ale must flow like the Thames."

"Perhaps also flagons of hard cider and mead. We have many artisanal distillers hereabouts."

"Jolly!"

♫**John Adams lies here, of the parish of Southwell/ A carrier who carried his can to his mouth quite well…** ♫

"And of course your staff will be appropriately liveried, I trust."

"Livers are our specialty, Vickers. Ha, ha. Rest assured, our staff will be suitably suited and bloody."

"Capital."

Mamie again sighed. Her son was so like a louder version of how his father had once been: young, naive, idealistic, and inclined to overreach.

"All most reassuring, Chef Algernon. May I trouble you further for recommendation of a talent agency. We shall be wanting a full ensemble of mummers, minstrels, troubadours, jugglers, a jester of course, perhaps also a conjurer."

"I myself would be pleased to handle such bookings, for only a modest additional **fee, fie, fo, fum, I smell the blood of an English bum.**"

"Splendid. As I say, there must be no stinting of expense for this grand affair. What you Yanks call 'conspicuous consumption' of the *nouveau riches*—pardon my French—we Brits proudly call displays of largesse signifying lordship, or in this case 'ladyship'. On Thursday we celebrate investiture of a noble member of the fairer sex,"

"Dare I ask which member of which lady?"

"Well, no one is to know her identity in advance," said the Vickers woman in a lowered voice, "but in strictest confidence, the lady possibly known to you as a Ms. Goodrich…"

Mimi Goodrich Everheart!

"…shall be recognized as the Virgin…"

Virgin!

"…Baroness of Bridgewater Abbey."

Baroness!

Mamie bit her tongue, literally. With blood dripping onto the desk, she barely managed to get to her feet. Her former longtime friend-turned-current longtime nemesis had already achieved their once-shared ambition to marry a wealthy man, which was itself a bitter pill. And now the conniving bitch was to realize their once-shared dream of becoming a titled aristocrat.

God in Heaven, she hated Mimi Goodrich!

CHAPTER NINE

As Major Jesterson continued to nap in a guest bedroom, Mimi reclined on a chaise lounge in the mansion's mistress suite, awake but virtually still swooning. She had always sensed that blue blood pulsed in her veins. She had always instinctively known she was, by breeding, superior to others. She had never thought of lower-class human beings as in any way "fellow".

To the contrary, during her ill-fated return to her ancestral English homeland as an American *Kraft Cheese* debutante, for instance, while all the other girls had gone along with orchestral renditions of the dreary "Once there was a spot" song from *Camelot* for their presentations to Prince Andrew, she herself now fondly recalled her selection of the King Arthur-Queen Guinevere duet...

♫*What do the simple folk do/ To help them escape when they're blue?/ When they're beset and besieged/ The folk not noblessly obliged/ Oh, what do simple folk do?*♫

Not that she herself had ever pretended to care about the doings of common people. She was no more hypocritical than she was what some called "affected". Her snobbery was heartfelt and genuine to its core.

♫*Whistling seems to brighten their day/ That's what simple folk do/ So they say*♫

Her mother had taught her at a young age that it was unladylike to whistle, to hum, to chew gum, to enjoy behaving in such peasantry ways.

♫*What else do simple folk do/ To help them escape when they're blue?/ They sit around and wonder what royal folk do*♫

Noblesse oblige was not meant to be fun. Being someone of prominent social standing for common folk to look up to was an onerous responsibility. She had been called to duty by divine…

Tap. Tap. Tap.

"Beg pardon, Madam," said the major through the door. "Are you decent?"

Changing into the nun-like garb, Mimi rued her foolhardy mistake of wedding O.B. Everheart. Alas, she had just returned from her sabotaged debut in London. A hospital nurse had described the older man as a cattle baron. His initials were O.B.E. She was young and naive.

Now, only youngish, she had finally been recognized as a rightfully titled aristocrat. She would return to London in triumph as a notable figure of high society. She would mix with other members of her class at weekend country house parties. She would forgive-and-forget Charles' somewhat shabby, perhaps deserved treatment of his first wife and Camilla's hand in her predecessor's murder. She would…

Ugh, she would be weighed down—if only by unseemly marital association—by the continued existence of O.B. Everheart. If only…

Mimi departed the mistress suite. Looking down upon Major Jesterson as he awaited her on a midway landing of the grand Hall of Heraldry staircase, she again almost swooned. Upon joining him there…

"Bit of 'ard cheese," he said. "Though person *non grata* at the Jubilee, Prince Andrew sends 'is regrets. Not to worry. To do the investiture Honours—thanks to Queen Victoria's royal libido and fecundity—bound to find a suitable 'Anover or Saxe-Coburg family member 'ere in the colonies. Bob's your uncle, what?."

Mimi declared that Prince Andrew's presence would not be missed, not by her.

"Jolly!" said the major, with a swat of swagger stick to his thigh. "Now, onward and upward—or rather downward—to re'earsal for your big night," he said taking her hand in his. "I

suggest that you, Madam, will 'arken to the call of 'Er Majesty's stand-in and appear from your chambers dressed as a virgin in, say, a white nightgown. Descent to this landing will no doubt 'ave an appropriately sobering effect on guests already assembled below you on the saloon floor. You shall then…Well, assume my 'umble self to be your dubber and kindly kneel before me."

Looking up to the tall, handsome member of British arms towering above her, Mimi realized — despite his mustache, slicked back hair and belly bulge — the major's familiar resemblance was to her favorite celebrity, Sir Michael Caine. She had particularly adored the famous British actor's performance as a younger red-coated soldier in *The Man Who Would Be King*.

And the colorfully uniformed officer now in her presence was a real O.B.E. If only she had met him at the Camelot Ball in London, lo, those many years ago…

"On be'alf of 'Er Royal 'Ighness, Queen Elizabeth the Second, I dub thee, Lady Mimi Goodrich, Virgin Baroness of Bridgewater Abbey," he said, gently tapping her nose with his swagger stick. "Let no man undub she that 'as been so dubbed. Amen."

Back on her feet, but weak in the knees, "Please, Major, I would like you to officialy dub me with your stick for real on Thursday night."

"Honored by your request, Madam, but…Well, come to think of it, I _am_ an official representative of the Crown. I suppose… Jolly well, Madam. I shall be chuffed to do the rub-a-dub-dubbing!"

"And as an official representative of the Crown, please advise me, Major. If a prior, uh, connubial 'consort' of a baroness were to appear from her past, would such a man — though possibly low born — be entitled to a title?"

"'Fraid not, Madam. Except for HRH making the Duke of Edinburgh a Prince Phillip by royal decree, never 'eard of a title passing by wedlock from trouble to mate."

"Trouble?"

"Trouble-and-strife. Means a bloke's better 'alf, or 'wife'."

Oh.

"On the other 'and, Virgin Baroness of Bridgewater Abbey is an 'ereditary title established by Good King 'Enry. So yes, some lucky bugger who 'appened to 'ave 'ad your 'and would become a Virgin Baron by marriage alright."

Ugh. Even with a title, O.B. Everheart would still be old as dirt and common as pig tracks. By now he should have already had the decency to drop dead.

"Ah, Vickers, right on cue," said the major, as his aide-de-camp came bounding up the stairs to the landing, followed by his batman, Bates. "Per'aps you could now describe to Madam Goodrich the knees-up she will be'old in celebration of 'er investiture."

"Gladly, major," said the Vickers woman after catching her breath. "Trumpeteers will herald the newly dubbed baroness' descent onto the grand saloon floor, where she will be greeted by a rising of hosannas voiced by a host of choristers. As traditional, mummers in masks of various animals will prance about the table that shall present an Olde English Feast fit for the groaning board of King Henry VIII. Indeed, the buffet shall be prepared by—believe it or not—a London-trained Chef Algernon Motley, versed in medieval cuisine per *Dame Elinor Fettiplace's Receipt Book* and also a past chef at ..."

"Algernon 'The Bastard' Motley?!"

"He didn't say, nor did his mother, who serves as the kitchen clerk."

"No!" said Mimi, stomping a foot. "I will not have that low-born boy bred by a hotel waiter and that loose woman in this mansion!"

"Well then," said Vickers, looking to the major, "Chik-Fil-A is the only other local provisioner capable filling an order for seventy couples on short notice, so a feast of nuggets will have to suffice. And we will have to find another talent agent to arrange entertainment on short notice."

"Nuggets', Vickers? What in blazes…?"

"Animal innards, Major," said Bates. "Left-over scraps for peasants in backwater 'amlets around the world."

"No!" said Mimi, stomping her other foot. "I absolutely will not have innards fit for peasants served at my investiture feast. And music for dancing must be arranged," she added, batting her eyes at the handsome major, but…

Ten minutes later, determined to have neither "nuggets" nor chicken sandwiches served at her investiture feast—not to mention dancing cheek-to-cheek with the major—Mimi grudgingly agreed to the arrangements made by the aide-de-camp, and flirtatiously batted her eyes at the armed batman.

If only her low-born husband could be made to permanently disappear, becoming The Right Honorable Lady Jesterson, Virgin Baroness of Bridgewater Abbey would truly be a dream deservedly come true.

CHAPTER TEN

Knock. Knock. Knock.

Max got up from the kitchen table and rushed toward the front door. Mom had wanted him to have the kid over for supper, but with O.B. Everheart also at the table tonight, the situation was touchy.

Knock. Knock.

He opened the door and stepped out onto the front porch. The kid, all shined up and holding a bunch of flowers, stepped back a peg. Max accepted the bouquet, and on the down-low proceeded to give the young case report jotter the lowdown on what was up.

The client's murderous wife and her accomplice, Buford Bailey had brought in...

"Mayor Buford Bailey?!"

Yeah, the *femme fatale* and the town's main insurance salesman had brought in an out-of-town hitman—or rather, am out-of-town hitchick who traveled by handy hearse—to do the grisly wet work, Max reported.

"Mr. Buford Bailey, the rhino?!"

Max explained that he had picked up the killerette's scent at the Everheart mansion and tailed her to a joint on the edge of town. He had witnessed the deadly dame ankle into a Prairie Home Cafe, carrying a briefcase, to no doubt collect wads of unmarked bills and pick up possibly an untraceable meat cleaver. He had staked out the joint, but...

"Anyway, the point is that while the client admits that his Missus wants him to permanently disappear from her sight, he

is having a hard time swallowing the bitter truth that she and Bailey are plotting to make him permanently disappear six-feet-under in order to cash in on insurance. So Mom doesn't want anything said about the case that might upset the old codger."

"Got it," said the kid, snatching back the bouquet. "Mum's the word."

Inside the kitchen, Mom at first looked like she was seeing a ghost, then rushed at the barely teenaged kid and began to hug "the spitting image of my little Maxie".

"Yeah, if I didn't know better, I'd say this here pear-shaped calf is your own grandson, Queenie."

"Now, let's get you bad boys fed," said Mom, turning toward pots and pans on the stove. "Good food makes a good mood."

"That's why I call her Queenie," said Everheart. "Your mom's cooking makes a man feel like a king."

"Yeah, but the Hallmark Channel now has a whole series called *Gourmet Mysteries*," said Max after joining the old man at the table. "Good food and mood for murrrderrr go together like ham and red-eye gravy."

"That's because most case reports are both written up and read by broads," said the kid, now also seated. "At the big bookstore in Tulsa there's a whole section called 'Culinary Mysteries', with titles like *The Butter Did It, Murder and Marinara, Death by Dumpling, The Cereal Killers, It Canoli Be Murder* and *Double Truffle.* An overhead sign has a quote by a famous poet named Mr. W.H. Auden, who said: 'Murder is commoner among cooks than among members of any other profession.'"

"Mimi never did much cooking," said the endangered client.

"Probably half those books are fiction," Max opined. "Cookbooks full of recipes, sweetened by fake murrrderrrs to get other broads to buy them."

"Not necessarily, Mr. Maximo. Nero Wolfe was what they call a gourmand. In *Case of Too Many Cooks* he got fourteen rivals of a murdered chef into a room and tricked the guilty one into…"

"Shhh!" Max shushed, after a glance at O.B. Everheart, who seemed to have turned a little greenish around the gills for some

reason. And he was tired of the kid always bringing up Wolfe, who yeah, was said to have weighed a third of a ton, but was a lightweight private dick compared to Brad Runyon, the real Fat Man.

"Who needs the cases of Nero Wolfe, or fake murrrderrrs in cookbooks, when you've got real McCoys right under your nose," he then said. "Back in the post-*Noir*, right up the road in Tulsa, a woman named Nannie Doss confessed, well…

"A first husband ran off because he feared she would poison his food.

"A second husband in fact died from ingestion of rat poison.

"A third husband she met through a lonely hearts club died of apparent heart failure, but then his relatives also began to keel over and she walked away with all the insurance money.

"A fourth sucker also succumbed to poison after about a year of marriage.

"And a fifth hubby suddenly died on the day he had been declared heathy by doctors, which prompted an autopsy after a big insurance pay-off and…Bingo, arsenic.

"*Case of the Giggling Grandma*, they called it, when the merry widow took the stand and lightheartedly explained that her actions were inspired by her reading of so-called romance novels."

Though he'd had nothing to eat yet, O.B. Everheart seemed to gag once or twice on something.

"Yeah," said the kid, "and just last week a broad out in Oregon, who wrote romantic murder mysteries — one titled *The Wrong Husband* — and an online essay titled *How to Murder Your Husband*, was convicted of following her own 'recipe', so to speak."

"Well, I myself have read many a romance novel, cooked many a meatloaf, and — may the Mister rest in peace — I once had a husband," said Mom, putting plates of meatloaf, mashed potatoes and gravy on the table. "But no one has ever suspected me of murder, for heaven's sake."

"No, thanks, Queenie."

"But you said you were hungry enough to eat a horse, O.B."

"Not any more, thanks just the same."

"Accounts of fake murrrderrrs are not fit to be printed," said Max, raking the client's meatloaf, mashed potatoes and gravy onto his own plate, "not in my book."

After having a so-called Mystery Meat Pie at the Prairie Home Cafe for a mid-morning snack, and then ordering another—which had caused him to not notice the hitchick's fade—he had gone back to the joint for lunch when told Bailey was "out of town" for the day. Ingredients of the mix were still a mystery to him, but…His nostrils had been set aquiver and tingling as well at the delicate luscious smell. The flavor, fit for a king! Gosh, those pies were good. And yet, he himself was now again hungry enough to eat a horse.

"Fake murder cases jotted in cookbooks by broads are one thing, but I'm sure you well recall one fake murder well worth being written up and read, Mr. Maximo," said the kid between mouthfuls of meatloaf. "The one staged by Sherlock Holmes in *Case of The Final Problem* was a corker."

"Remind me."

Max had never quite mastered the brainy case reports jotted by a Dr. Watson.

"After surviving three attempts on his life by Professor Moriarty's henchmen in London, Mr. Sherlock met his evil nemesis in supposedly a fight to the death at Reichenbach Falls in the Switzerland mountains. Dr. Watson afterward deduced that both Mr. Sherlock and Moriarty had fallen to their deaths while locked in mortal combat."

"And the jotter got it wrong, right? See, kid, how many times do I have to tell you…"

"Yeah, I know: ' A-S-S-U-M-E makes M-E an A-S-S without U'. And you are right. Mr. Maximo. Dr. Watson literally fell to the ground when Mr. Sherlock showed up three years later in *Case of The Empty House*; alive and well but still pursued by a vengeful Moriarty thug. Remember how Mr. Sherlock outwitted him?"

"Remind me."

"He put a fake dummy of himself in the window of 221B Baker Street, and lay in wait across the street. Sure enough, the would-be hitman fell for it, and got caught red-handed after firing a deadly air gun at the dummy."

Hmmm. Max's brain, which he often thought of as a hamster inside his head, began to spin.

"And in a somewhat similar situation down in Houston, Texas, a few years ago—the one in which a guy taped his wife plotting with a hitman on the phone…"

"At least have a little dessert, O.B. I made these myself to practice for a church cooking club contest to mark the upcoming National Donut Day."

"No thanks, Miz Morgan. I think I'll just go to bed."

With the client up and gone from the table, "See what you bad boys have done?" Mom hissed. "You've worried poor Mr. Everheart to death."

Mom was almost always right, and in fact—though neither he nor the kid had said a word about *Case of the Baron and the Old Bimbo*—the client had looked like a proverbial dead-man-walking when he retired for the night and…

As the kid went on with details of the Houston case—accompanied now by the sound of O.B. Everheart vomiting inside a bathroom down a hall — the hamster coughed up a plan to kill two birds with one rock.

WEDNESDAY

June 4, 2022

CHAPTER ELEVEN

Max stood at the Mr. Quickie pick-up counter with a hand out. Quickie gave him a fish eye, but forked over his camera phone and a printed photo without comment. The deal that allowed him to private dick in a copy shop workstation cubicle had a condition attached to it. No pornographic materials such as sometimes cropped up from surveillance in marital disputes were permitted on the premises.

No *problemo*. Every shamus worth his gumshoes—from Mike Hammer to Sam Spade to Jessica Fletcher to Yours Truly—avoided penny-ante divorce cases at almost all costs. Cases of possible murrrderrr, however, were different kettles of fish.

Ankling down Main Street with the camera phone in hand and the photo tucked into a jacket pocket, he debated with himself whether to spell out appearances or let the picture by itself do the talking.

In *Case of Double Indemnity*, the merry widow was in a hurry to get her mitts on the insurance bucks, but the insurance salesman got cold feet when he realized a savvy company inspector smelled a rat. So he wanted to play it cool; not rush filing for the pay-out for bumping off the *femme fatale's* husband. That was why the flim-flammer finally shot his co-conspirator—not because he had a soft spot for her stepdaughter—only after she had already plugged him for getting in her way to Easy Street.

Buford Bailey, on the other hand—unlike his counterpart in the *Case of Double Indemnity* who did the wet work with his own hands—didn't have that reason to take down Mimi Everheart,

at least not yet. But if, or rather when the deadly dame's husband appeared to permanently disappear under suspicious circumstances, it would be every man for him-and-herself, Max was thinking when he arrived out front of Bailey's insurance agency and…

Before he had decided how to play his hole card, the suspect came out the door, bumped into him and said: "Sorry, Max, I'm in a hurry. Go inside and state your business to my assistant. She will take care of…"

"My business is with you, Buster," said Max, reaching for the photo with one hand and holding up the camera phone with the other.

"It's 'Booster', not 'Buster', but…Holy cow, is that O.B. Everheart?" said the mope, staring at the photo as Max clicked pics. "Over seventy years old, and still sleeping with a stuffed teddy bear?"

His plan — based on trickeration used by cops in the Houston case reported by the kid last night — was to record the perp's guilty reaction when faced with staged evidence that the hitchick he'd hired…

"What's that coming out of O.B.'s ear? Looks like… barbecue sauce?"

Dog-gone-it, he'd been afraid chilled catsup from the fridge would wake the sleeping client, so now had to spell it out. "Looks like drying blood to me, which is why I came by to handle a life insurance claim for our mutual client."

"O.B. Everheart is d-d-d-dead?"

"D-D-D-Dead as Disco by the look of him."

"Has Mi-Mi-Mimi been told by…anyone?"

"That's your job, Bailey. Let's take a ride."

Though making excuse after excuse for why he should not have to be the one to break "b-b-b-bad news to the poor widow", Bailey came along peaceably. But then, from the boiler's shotgun seat…

"If it was death by accident, the company will have to pay double indemnity," the scam artist admitted. "If it was death by

suicide, the company won't pay a dime, but will take the trouble-and-expense of dealing with a disappointed widow out on me for not spotting signs of an attempt scam. Let's hope for the best that…"

"Yeah, let's hope it was murrrderrr."

"M-M-M-Murrrderrr? Oh my God, Mimi will be…"

"Yeah, the wife—and a certain chummy 'friend'—will be suspects *Numero Uno* and *Tuo*. Wandering spouses and lovers are always pegged as most likely the doers in triangle cases, especially when an insurance salesman is involved. Ever see the documentary film about *Case of Double Indemnity*?"

At his mention of the famous case—intended to crack the yardbird like a softboiled egg—Bailey instead went quiet as a… as a hardboiled egg, but….Dog-gone-it. At the wheel of the boiler, he himself was unable to snap a pic of the quilty look on the insurance salesman's sweating face.

Max made a mental note to not again make the mistake of tipping his hand too soon, and put pedal to the metal.

A doll dressed like a cafe waitress came to the door of the Everheart mansion, but said the madam of the house was not entertaining guests at the moment. He put her wise to the emergency and waved a light green refresher. Bingo. She led them in, and then out of the fancy digs, to a flower garden, where…

♫**…thy hope is crowned/ God made thee mightier yet/ On sov'ran brows, beloved, renowned/ Once more thy crown is set…**♫

"With respect, Madam, simply the tune of *Pomp and Circumstance* might best suit," a waiter in a red coat was saying, apparently about music coming from one of those flip-top computers that sat on a table.

"But Vickers said there would be choristers," said a dark-haired dame at the table—obviously the flat-chested *femme fatale* herself—already dressed like a black widow in fake mourning. "A sing-along would be fun."

♫**God, who made thee mighty, make thee mightier yet…**♫

"I doubt guests will be familiar with the lyrics, Madam. Sing-along of another song more appropriate for the occasion will…"

"Pardon, Ms. Ever, uh, Ms. Goodrich," the waitress shouted. "Mr. Bailey and a fat man are here to see you about a double indemnity insurance scam."

The red-coated yardbird stopped the music. The *femme fatale* swiveled her head and…With the element of surprise off the table, so to speak, Max ankled into the game, showed his down-and-dirty hole card, and said: "Read 'em and weep, 'Ms.' Ever, uh, Goodrich'."

"What on earth?…Oh my God, it's, uh… Dead to the world and smeared with…Ugh, steak sauce. I have told that old fool a hundred times that it is uncouth to eat dinner in bed and…Ugh. As a religious vegetarian, I regard this disgusting display of meat consumption as evidence of outright murder."

"You said it, Sisterrr," said Max, pointing the camera phone.

"I'm so so-so-sorry, Mimi," said Bailey, wringing his hands.

"'Oo is this dead meat?" said the red-coated waiter, peering over "Madam's" shoulder.

"Uh, uh, not to worry, Major. This uncouth old fool is O.B. Everheart, just, uh, an acquaintance," said the black widow.

"O.B. Ever'eart is brown bread?! Oo's to provide the 'oney—meaning money—for the rites of investiture?!"

"Don't worry about funeral expenses, Mimi," said Bailey, taking his accomplice's hand in his and no doubt covertly squeezing. "It was obviously an accident. Just look at that smile on O.B.'s face. Double indemnity will more than…We should sit down and talk about a policy that will cover your own valuable ass…"

As Max took pictures of the *femme fatale's* also smiling face… Uh oh. None other than the hitchick brazenly barged into the flower garden, followed by a thug wearing a red cap, bandolier of ammo strapped across his chest, and a holstered Roscoe on his hip.

"Let's get down to the hangers-on list," said the hired killer he had tailed to the Mystery Meat Pie cafe, as she dealt a sheet of paper onto the table. "Mr. Quickie needs to start printing

personalized invitations by noon if they are to be ready for delivery tomorrow morning."

Max peered over the black widow's shoulder and read:

HEAR YE! HEAR YE! HEAR YE!

SAVE THE DATE
Thursday, June 3, 2022…6:00 P.M.…Althorp House II

FESTIVE RITES OF INVESTITURE

All-You-Can-Eat Olde English Buffet…Free Beverages for All

Music and Dance

Jousters…Jesters…Jugglers

Special Sing-A-Long!

JOIN THE JUBILEE!

By Personal Invitation Only…Semi-Formal (Shoes & Shirts)
Max had encountered plenty of *femmes fatale* in pulp case reports and documentary films through the years—from Charlotte Manning in Mike Hammer's *Case of I, The Jury*, to Brigid O'Shaughnessy in Sam Spade's *Case of The Maltese Falcon*, to Phyllis What's-Her-Name in *Case of Double Indemnity*—but for crying out loud, this deadly dame took the cake.

Even before seeing the doctored evidence that the body of her doting husband was dropping below room temperature, Mimi Everheart had already started planning a party to celebrate "investiture" of his remains six feet into a hole—as the saying went—where the sun didn't shine.

Realizing he was up against a stone-cold band of killers not likely to blink at sight of his Roscoe, Max faded from the flower garden like a wilting weed that had got a whiff of *Round Up*.

CHAPTER TWELVE

♫**Five little ducks went out one day/ Over the hills and far away/ Mother duck said, 'quack, quack, quack, quack'/ Only four little ducks came back...** ♫

As Algie loudly sang an olde English children's song while working in the adjacent kitchen, Mamie again sat at her office desk, counting cash outlays for the so-called feast for so-called "investiture" of that so-called virgin, Mimi Goodrich Everheart.

♫**Four little ducks went out one day/ Over the hills and far away/ Mother duck said, 'quack, quack, quack'/ Only three little ducks came back...** ♫

Her son had already harvested the properly fatted ducks in his flock. Now he was pushing the envelope by butchering younger ducks that had been overfed with corn for fewer than three weeks. And even that drastic move, Mamie feared, would not be enough.

♫**Three little ducks went out one day/ Over the hills and far away/ Mother duck said, 'quack, quack'/ Only two little ducks came back...** ♫

Fatty duck livers were the essential ingredient of Algie's Secret Sauce, without which most if not all of so-called "artisanal' Prairie Home Meats dishes were—frankly—not fit to eat.

♫**Two little ducks went out one day/ Over the hills and far away...** ♫

Livers from other sources had been ordered—and paid for—at an exorbitant cost. And still the supply might be thin for the Olde English feast the company was committed to provide.

♫**One little duck went out one day/ Over the hills and far away/ Mother duck said, 'quack'/ No little duck came back** ♫

And Secret Sauce, though indispensable, would not itself make a feast. Mutton was plentiful and cheap, but swans were off the table. Market conditions were also tight for prairie oysters, stags, hogs' heads; and Tots Lyon was no fool. The only dependable jester within three hundred miles was holding out for double his usual fee. At the price quoted to that British woman, the company would be lucky to break even, even if…

Mamie got up from the desk and stormed into the kitchen.

"Simple Simon met a pieman, going to the fair/ Said Simple Simon to the pieman, 'Let me taste your ware…'"

"Algie, we need to talk!" she semi-shouted at her son, who hovered over a large pot with blood up to his elbows.

"Said the pieman to Simple Simon, 'Show me first your penny…"

"Algie!"

"No need to shout, Mother. I heard you clacking on that old subtracting machine. But not to worry. Simply go to the client on bended knee and get more money. The swells must eat, drink and be merry, for tomorrow they shall…"

Mamie turned on a heel and bolted from the kitchen. Her usually impractical son and business partner had unwittingly given her a possibly life-saving idea. She would unreasonably demand down payment of at least sixty percent of the agreed total price. The Vickers woman would reasonably reject the demand. Prairie Home Company catering of tomorrow's scheduled event would be canceled, and Mimi Goodrich Everheart's elevation to titled virgin would be celebrated, if at all, with a feast of food and drink provided by, say, Burger King.

At the wheel of the company's second-hand van, she relished the prospect of ruining Mimi's party, perhaps in a gratifying face-to-face encounter. They had caught sight of one another from time to time, but had not spoken — nor even acknowledged each other's existence — for almost thirty years. Needless to say, she had never been inside "Althorp House II", a pile of stones

supposedly modeled after part of Princess Diana's ancestral home in England, but looking more like…Well, in the words of one local wag, the replica of only the middle section of the original Althorp House reminded one of a fat nesting goose with its wings cut off.

Nearing the "goose", Mamie noticed that an old brown car had been driven into a roadside ditch, but…No, she was in too much of a hurry to rescue the fat man waving for help.

Entering the Althorp House II circular driveway, it barely registered as odd that a parked black vehicle adorned with little British flags appeared to be a somewhat battered hearse.

At the pseudo-mansion's massive front door, she stated her business to a friend's young daughter—working as a housemaid—who led her into an open-air courtyard. Mimi—dressed as a nun, no doubt to suggest "virginhood"—sat at a table, flanked for some reason by Mayor Bailey on one side, holding her hand, and by Ms. Vickers on the other side, holding a pen.

"…but the Leonards are lower class," the lady of the big house was saying. "The Mister hales from the state's wretched panhandle region."

"There's no need for you to personally fancy every invited guest, Madam. We are now halfway through the local voter rolls and have identified…Let's see, two, four…only eight 'friends'."

"The old judge won't likely eat or drink much," said the Mayor, "but that wife of his…"

"Pardon, Ms. Ever…er, Ms. Goodrich. Ms. Motley won't go away until you pay a bill."

To judge by the look on Mimi's face, one might have thought the Grim Reaper had called upon her for settlement of accounts, but…

"Ah, Ms. Mamie," said the ever-orangish Mayor, grinning like an out-of-season jack-o-lantern. "How timely. See, Mimi, another friend to add to the guest list."

Mimi's glare at His Honor would have frozen a side of beef.

"I will discuss feast particulars with you and Chef Algernon privately, Ms. Motley," said the prissy female British agent. "Until then…"

Mimi turned away her head. Gazing at a courtyard blank wall, "Did I not make it clear that the help is not to be gadding about inside my mansion?"

"Technically speaking, this is an outdoor courtyard, Madam."

Mamie stated her business to Ms. Vickers. Unless she received immediate payment of seventy-five percent of the agreed catering price of $225-a-head for one-hundred and forty…

Mini swiveled her head with a jerk. "I shall authorize a stipend for kitchen help in such amount at such time as strictly *noblesse obliged*."

"Well then, sorry to rain on your parade, Mimi, but…"

"Parade?" said Ms. High-and-Mighty, with a bright-eyed turn of her head to Ms. Vickers.

"A figure of speech, Madam. No doubt Ms. Motley means that unless immediately paid, she will not cater your Feast of Investiture. Time is quite short, and I fear…"

"You planned to sabotage my investiture all along, didn't you, Mamie Motley!" the baroness-to-be screeched face-toface. "Just like you ruined the *Kraft Cheese* presentation of debutantes to high society at the Camelot Ball!"

"It was <u>you</u>, my dear Ms. 'Ever, uh, Goodrich', who was forced to leave the ball, literally 'slipperless' and then some, after your botched curtsy to Prince Andrew."

"My curtsy was not 'botched', I'll have you know. It was intentional slapstick to protest the shabby treatment of Princess Diana by Andrew's formerly odious brother."

"By falling to your knees and thrusting your face into his royal crotch?!"

"I stumbled, but made my point. They asked him to leave too, as you may recall."

"Oh yes, I still have photos of the unfortunate incident, 'Milady Mimi, Baroness of Bilgewater Abbey'."

"Out with this strumpet!" the unwanted catering client shouted, rising from her chair like a black storm cloud. "I will not have this gossipy trollop and her bastard son in or out of Althorp House Number Two!"

Stomping from the courtyard through the house, Mamie's own rage was momentarily interrupted by glimpse of a tall red-coated man darting across a hallway. Outside, getting into the parked van, she had to remind herself that her mission had been successful. The company would suffer a significant but survivable loss, and Algie would be sorely disappointed, but...

"Yoohoo, Ms. Motley."

Ms. Vickers ran toward her, waving something in her hand.

"Terribly sorry about the bit of bother," the British woman said. "As an American colonist, Madam Goodrich has not yet mastered the aristocratic manner of not noticing those beneath notice of their betters."

"Maybe so, but not noticing the server of Burger King onion rings at her feast-for-friends might be hazardous to the health of her and her guests."

"Oh no, never Burger King. The major and I stand by the Crown Chancery's commitment," said Vickers holding out what looked to be a credit card. "Please accept full payment in advance, remain calm, and carry on as agreed."

Printed on the *Mastercard* was the name *O. B. Everheart*, Mini's reputedly doting and reliably credit-worthy husband.

"In deference to the whims of the presumptive baroness, however, the major and I must require, per protocol, that the help—other than liveried table attendants—confine yourselves to the kitchen during the investiture feast-and-frolic."

In part hating herself, Mamie tucked the credit card into a shirt pocket and got into the company van. Driving back toward the Prairie Home Meats & Cafe kitchen, an Olde English nursery song came to mind:

♫*Soldier, Soldier, won't you marry me/ with your musket, fife and drum/ Oh no, sweet maid, I cannot marry you/ for a have not trousers on.*

Soldier, Solider, won't you marry me… ♫

How strange. Glimpse of the hurried red-coated man had momentarily taken her back to London more than thirty years ago…

♫*Oh no, sweet maid, I cannot marry you/ for I have a wife at home* ♫

…where and when she met the englishman in similar uniform who would become Algie's father.

CHAPTER THIRTEEN

Max drove the now slightly dented brown boiler onto the driveway of the house that had been his home base since birth. Gently, he braked the vehicle to a stop, tumbled out, and with head down, crawled toward the house's back door. In flight from the gang of ghouls gathered at the Everheart mansion, he had made the mistake of looking back over his shoulder and…For crying out loud, no one would help him get the boiler out of a roadside ditch until he called the kid, who came up with the idea of contacting AAA for a tow job.

But the bloodthirsty gang would be coming after him. There was no doubt about that.

Inside the house, he stood up, locked the door behind him, put his fedora on a hook and…Yeah, just as he had expected: Mom sat at the kitchen table, looking across a checkers board for the man who wasn't there: his client, O.B. Everheart.

"Where on Earth have you been?" Mom asked. "And where is O.B.?"

He put a finger to his lips to shush her, then moved to a window and closed the curtains. In a whisper, he explained that he got up early, paused only for a sack of donuts, and had to tie-up his phone almost constantly in order to trap the client's killers.

"Killers?! Oh my God, it's your fault, Max. Last night at supper, you and that smart-alecky look-alike kid scared that poor old man half to death with tales of wives murdering husbands!"

Mom was almost always right—maybe the kid had in fact flushed the sitting duck into the open—but now was not

the time for pointing fingers. Now was the time to go to the mattresses.

"No, no napping, Max. O.B. may have made a run for it and got away. He may have gone back to the Fountainblue Motel for his truck and…"

Knock. Knock-Knock. Knock.

Max again shushed his mom, took Old Junior from its shoulder holster, went to the back door and waited.

Knock. Knock-Knock. Knock…**Knock! Knock!**

"I got over here on my bike as soon as I could after finishing breakfast and cleaning up my room, Mr. Maximo," said the kid, rushing inside. "What's up?"

In more detail than circumstances had allowed by phone and circumstances, Max put the kid and his mom wise to what had gone down. Bottom line: Bailey and the *femme fatale* had as much as copped to their plot when confronted with the fake photo, but…

"You poured steak sauce into O.B.'s ear?! Shame on you, Max! That poor old man must have woke up, scared to…He must have tried to make it to the hospital."

"No way, Mom. With my own peepers I saw the look in the eyes of the hitchick and armed thug when they reported back to the *femme fatale*. I got a pic of the smile on the *femme's* face when she eyeballed my photo. For crying out loud, they had already started setting up investiture of the client's remains. And…"

"'Investiture'?"

"…you know who's next on their list."

"Who?" said the kid, with notebook and pencil now in hand.

"The guy who knows too much."

"Who would that be, Mr. Maximo?"

"Yours Truly, that's who. We've got to go to the mattresses."

"Shouldn't we call in the cops first?" said the kid.

"Yes, report to Chief Potter," said Mom. "And on the way to police headquarters, see if O.B.'s truck is gone from the motel parking lot. I'll call the hospital."

After arguing against making a wrong move in plain sight, Max reluctantly shuffled toward the door. To be on the safe-as-possible side, he told the kid to follow him on his bike, and handed over his fedora. Inside the boiler, he retrieved his own disguise from the glove compartment. Off they went.

Mike Hammer had the benefit of a sometimes touchy, but basically okay working relationship with Lieutenant Pat Chambers of the New York City Police Department. Sam Spade had the benefit of being buddy-buddy with Detective Tom Polhaus of the Frisco P.D. Same for Phillip Marlowe and Chief Inspector Bernie Ohis in L.A. Yours Truly, on the other hand, had always been at the disadvantage of gumshoeing in a backwater burg where badged flatfooting was in the incompetent hands-and-feet of a nine-to-five donutter named Pete Potter.

Potter was a paper-pusher; picky as a peacock about being called "Pete" instead of "Pat", and a stickler for going page-by-page by the book. Yeah, curling up by a fire and reading fake murder mysteries was Potter's kind of lay. In *Case of the Jealous Strawberry Blonde*, for instance, it had been like pulling teeth to get the slow-footed fake Jake to dredge Lake Henryetta for a body that…Okay, only the half-eaten corpse of an unusually large catfish had turned up. The strawberry blonde *femme fatale* skated. And since then the *faux* Five-O and he had seen eye-to-eye, so to speak, only when butting heads. But to satisfy Mom…

Max parked the boiler at a Main Street curb, checked his disguise in the rearview mirror, and slunk into police headquarters. Instead of at his desk, as usual, Potter happened to be manning the station's stand-up counter, shuffling paper as usual.

"Pssst!" Max hissed, to get the chief clerk's attention.

"What's up with the fake eyeglasses and fake plastic nose, Morgan, not to mention the black eyebrows and mustache?"

"Keep it on the down-low, Pete," Max whispered. "If asked by a dame who speaks English, I was never here. Got it?"

"I wish."

Max reached into a pants pocket, pulled out the camera phone and held it up. "What do you see on this mope's face, Potter? Any sign of guilt?"

"I see Buford Bailey, looking semi-puzzled by something in his hand."

"Max flicked to the picture of Mimi Everheart's reaction to the staged photo of her husband. "And what do you see on this dame's face? Puzzlement?"

"I see Mrs. Everheart looking down at something, surprised, and smiling like she just got a birthday present."

Aha! Max reached into a jacket pocket, pulled out the staged photo and slapped the graphic evidence onto the counter.

"This is what Bailey and the Everheart broad were looking at when I caught them on candid camera, Potter. Now, tell me what you see that would be so 'puzzling' to someone?"

"I see Old Man Everheart with steak sauce in his ear, smiling like he's about to break out laughing."

"What makes you think that's not blood coming out of his ear?"

"Well, for one thing, there's a bottle of *Country Bob's Original Steak Sauce* sitting there on what looks to be a nightstand. For another…"

Max snatched the photo from the counter. Dog-gone-it… "Looks like drying blood to me. To the wife, if not the insurance salesman, it no doubt looked like O.B. Everheart is dead as Kelsey's nuts."

"So what do you want me to do, 'Fat Mannn'? Put a 'collar' on Country Bob for murder by sauce?"

Max spelled out what had gone down — namely coldblooded murrrderrr — and what was up — namely another coldblooded murrrderrr of Yours Truly-- if the Barney Fife didn't hotfoot out to the Everheart mansion and…

"As a matter of fact, the wife picked up a 'Save the Date' flyer. So yeah, Morgan, if we get an invitation, I'll be sure to 'hotfoot' out there tomorrow night for the 'Jubilee'. Maybe you'll get

lucky and be invited. There's to be an All-You-Can-Eat Buffet that sounds right down your alley."

Max was surprised. Though Potter was dumb as a sack of nails, he had not pegged the town's chief badge as necessarily bent.

On the other hand, he was not shocked. Mimi Everheart would soon be rolling in life insurance dough, if not a large inheritance. Her accomplice, Bailey, was the burg's Mayor, likely already sweetening the phoney flatfoot's pot of perks on a Town Hall back burner.

And the meat pie was already half-baked, so to speak. Unless he found a way to turn off the gas, next would come a topping of real "secret sauce" made from the grisly remains of Yours Truly.

CHAPTER FOURTEEN

♫*I was beat, incomplete/ I'd been had, I was sad and blue/ But you made me feel/ Yeah, you made me feel, shiny and new...* ♫

With Madonna's classic musical ode to self-reinvention running through her head, Mini discarded the drab nun-like garb she had been wearing since yesterday. From a dressing room drawer, she plucked a white negligee more suitable for tomorrow night's *fete*.

♫*I made it through the wilderness/ Somehow I made it through/ Didn't know how I lost I was/ Until I found you...* ♫

For her investiture, Major Jesterson would receive her on the landing of the Hall of Heraldry's "apples-and-pears"—his quaint term for stairs—and take her hand. She would drop to her knees. He would dub her with his swagger stick...

♫*Like a virgin/ Touched for the very first time...* ♫

In the meantime, there were other matters to attend to. Temporarily missing the big picture, the major had been visibly upset by the photo brought to her by the ever-reliable Buford Bailey—accompanied by a fat man later identified as a detective—showing her husband to be "brown bread". To her surprise, the major had asked "Oo was to pay" for the feast celebrating her official elevation into even higher upper-class; and then—much to her distress—rushed off to call Chancery "eadquarters" about "funding".

Adding to the taint of middle-class commercial crassness, the morning had been further marred by the uninvited and unwelcome appearance of that still blonde, still blue-eyed, still disgustingly big-bosomed bimbo—Mamie Motley—daring to

set foot on the premises of Althorp House II, with the gall to demand payment for the privilege of catering tomorrow night's feast.

Mimi sighed. Admittedly, she herself had struggled to maintain aristocratic indifference to the lowly person and her petty concerns. Only after the cutlery maid had been dismissed—and the major returned to urgently urge that she accept practical considerations of the circumstances—did she graciously acquiesce to maintenance of arrangements for feast food service by Mamie Motley and the illegitimate offspring of a mere hotel waiter.

Now seated at a vanity and applying a bit of rouge to her cheeks…Hmmm, Mimi was struck by a notion that the deposed childhood beauty queen and her bastard son might still attempt to somehow spitefully ruin her triumph. Reminded that uneasy rests the crown, she bravely again sighed.

Later the major had explained, to her surprise, that it was customary for newly titled nobility to pick up the tab for private parties in their own honor; and furthermore—to her shock—that the Virgin Baroness of Bridgewater Abbey estate, as a religious institution dependent on alms from the poor, would be neither allowed nor able to foot the bill for tomorrow night's "knees up".

Dear dependable Buford had immediately comforted both of them by confirming that in addition to a large inheritance under O.B. Everheart's last will and testament, she would be collecting "double indemnity" insurance proceeds when her prior mate's permanent disappearance was officially determined to have been accidental, as would undoubtedly prove to be the case.

Indeed, as a religious vegetarian, she thought it only fitting that the old cow puncher, his hands bloody from slaughter of cattle by the thousands, would choke to death on a chunk of dead meat.

"Let's 'ave a bubble," the major had said, meaning champagne, she had thought, though he had already filled Diana's wine glass with whiskey. "Means let's 'ave a 'bubble bath'," he had further

explained. Though embarrassed by the bold proposition made in the presence of the others, she had been inclined to discreetly accept, but… "Means let's 'ave a laugh," he said, before finishing a "tumble-down-the-sink", meaning his drink.

In the course of later conversation, she had come to understand Major Jesterson's refined British way of speaking, though possibly not *vice versa*.

During lunch, he said he did not believe a word of the caterer's "weep-and-wail" passed on by Ms. Vickers, by which he meant he put no credence in the "tale" told by Mamie Motley about her slapstick curtsy to Prince Andrew at the Camelot Ball. And "'ow" convenient that she was not currently a "cows-and-kisses", he said, meaning that he was pleased she was not a "Missus".

Furthermore, he had described as "'ow" inconvenient for her lineage it was that she had no "dustbins-and-lids"—meaning kids—except for "'er late 'usband's 'bricks-and-mortar", meaning her stepdaughter. In answer to her asking, she was relieved to be told that no, her hereditary title as Virgin Baroness of Bridgewater Abbey would not pass to the conniving little stepbitch who might otherwise plot against her.

Between rounds of "pigs-and-roasts" to the Queen on the upcoming occasion of Her Majesty's Platinum Jubilee, and repeated visits to the "loo" to "spend a penny", the dashing British military officer had repeatedly complimented her on her "fanny", meaning the passionate nature she brought to the occasion.

After the others had left the table, Mimi had subtly hinted to Major Jesterson that comfort of his private company would not be unwelcome, but…Seeming to have "lost the plot", he too had staggered off to "Bedfordshire"—meaning the guest bedroom assigned to him—for a nap, but…

Tap. Tap. Tap.

"Are you decent, Mimi?

Drat! It was only Buford tapping. Throughout lunch the insurance salesman had repeatedly interrupted her conversation with the major to offer laughable advice that she should sign

up for life insurance that would secure her inheritable assets for Sugar.

Annoyed by his idiotic suggestion and persistence, she now picked up her phone, punched his number, and said: "No, I am not decent. And you should be tending to matters downtown by now."

"Roger. Just dropped by to confirm that Ms. Vickers, Corporal Bates and I are on our way to make discreet inquiries and arrangements about…"

"Again, confide in no one who might pass on disturbing gossip to Sugar!"

"No, of course not, Mimi. As you said, yesterday, there is no reason to upset the dear girl until absolutely necessary."

Mimi ended the call, but…

Buzz. Buzz. Buzz.

Speak of the little she-devil… "Sugar, my dear, glad you called," she said into her phone. "You must stay with your fat aunt until Sunday night at least. I doing some things with the mansion."

"I'm not in Tulsa with Aunt Peg. I'm here, with Algie. And I am never coming back to that house as long as you are alive."

Mimi ground her teeth.

"I called to tell you that I know what you're up to, Mimi. I know what you have always been up to. But it won't work. You won't get away with it this time."

Buzzzzzz.

Mimi sighed. As a young girl, she herself had longed for a higher-class maternal figure in her life. Unlike other girls who, for instance, warmly related to the lowly and conniving milkmaid in *The Sound of Music*, she had thought Baron Von Trapp was foolish to reject his fiancee—who was already a titled baroness in her own right—simply because the refined lady quite understandably wanted to send the baron's seven noisy brats away to boarding school.

Like most silly young girls, however, Sugar's feeble mind had been indelibly impressed by the virtues and vices of stereotypical

characters portrayed in fairytales such as *Cinderella, Snow White* and the like. To correct such biased profiling, she—as a dutiful stepmother—had long ago assigned to the troubled child an essay by an expert on the female psyche, namely a man named Garrison Keillor, who had brilliantly "deconstructed" those biased myths of white fairy godmother superiority.

In the piece titled *My Stepmother, Myself*, the author had more realistically pointed out that Snow White's stepmother had only tried to protect her from Prince Charming, who was, after all, a necrophiliac. Also that Cinderella would likely have come to later realize her stepmother had her best interests at heart in teaching her the virtues of hard work.

But oh no, Sugar's favorite unreconstructed fairytale became one titled *The Rose-Tree*, in which a supposedly "wicked" stepmother—who cut off the head of a no doubt incorrigible stepdaughter, stewed her heart and liver and fed the girl's organs to her father—got her "just deserts" when an angry bird dropped a millstone on <u>her</u> head. Thanks to such dangerous so-called "critical theory" fed to the impressionable child, selfless service as Sugar's stepmother had been a thankless task.

Mimi again sighed; dabbed some color onto her lips, and—with the coast clear—got up from the vanity.

♫*I made it through the wilderness/ Somehow I made it through...* ♫

At the bedroom door, she momentarily trembled. Down a hallway leading to guest bedrooms, she paused at the head of the grand staircase, looked down into Heraldry Hall, and...

♫*Didn't know how lost I was/ Until I found you...* ♫

...there he was, Major Lawrence Jesterson, slouched in a chair set at the Hall's long banquet table...his flaming red coat unbuttoned...a shirttail hanging out from out of his trousers... one bare foot on the table...looking up to her.

♫*Oh, your love thawed out/ Yeah, your love thawed out/ What was getting cold* ♫

"Madam, pray take a lump-of-ice from Smokey the Bear", he shouted, meaning "take a word of advice", "to-wit: Be sure to

put on knickers under the nightgown tomorrow night, lest the 'eraldry 'all torches start a brush fire."

"It's too late!" she boldly shouted back. "You, Sir, have already enflamed my passionate fanny!

Mimi again trembled as her handsome suitor struggled to his feet with possibly Princess Diana's now half-filled wine glass fittingly in hand…lurched to the staircase… climbed a few steps and…to her horror, dropped the treasured wine glass, collapsed upon the apples-and-pears, and…to her dismay, immediately began to loudly snore.

♫*Like a virgin…* ♫

CHAPTER FIFTEEN

Back behind the wheel of the brown boiler, Max looped wide around the north edge of town, as far away as possible from the southside Everheart mansion, where he would again be outnumbered and outgunned by a mob that made the Mafia look like a girl-and-boy scout troop.

With a bull's eye right between his eyes, it was risky to even be out and about in late afternoon daylight, but risky business was the lay of a private eye with a dead client. In the eyes of his own mom, he was responsible—along with the kid—for the rub-out of O.B. Everheart. To boot, he had looked the old man in the eye and promised he would keep an eye on not only his Missus, but also the daughter who was the apple of his eye.

Yeah, the "eyes" had it, so to speak, by a clear majority. His handling of *Case of the Baron and the Old Bimbo* was a black eye on the profession of private dickery.

Returned home from police headquarters following his head-butting with Potter, he'd been not surprised by his mom's report that the client had not shown up at the hospital. Neither had he been surprised by the kid's report that Everheart's truck was not in the Fountainblue parking lot. No way could the old codger have made it on foot to either place; not on a hot summer day; not after being fitted for a wooden overcoat by the hitchick and shoved into the backend of a hearse by her co-thug. The dirty deed was done. And the fix was in at Town Hall.

After a late lunch of kibble biscuits and water in the kitchen of Mom's doghouse, there had seemed to be nothing more to do

except go to the mattresses and look out for Number One, but then...

"Too bad Mr. Everheart didn't have a daughter," the kid had said from the other twin bed, where O.B. Everheart had bunked the night before. His case jotter had gone on to remind him that in *Case of Double Indemnity*, a stepdaughter was onto the *femme fatale* for murdering her biological mother years earlier. Unfortunately, the unsavvy doll had made the mistake of taking her hunch to the insurance salesman; but at least the move turned the mope against his co-conspirator by...

Bingo. He had not bothered to pass on the skinny that the victim in *Case of the Baron and the Old Bimbo* had a youngish daughter named Sugar. He'd not thought the detail was worth mentioning. But as the kid went on re-telling that the insurance salesman in the *Case of Double Indemnity* had got sweet on that case's *femme fatale's* stepdaughter, a play had hit him in the gut like a pang of hunger.

His mom often said sugar was a better than vinegar for catching flies. And Mom was almost always right. Okay, lose some, win some; that was how the gumshoe game went. Now what he had in mind was a new play, simple as a piece of cake, or rather simple as downing another Mystery Meat Pie, Max was thinking, as he steered the boiler into the Prairie Home Cafe parking lot.

Inside the joint, he ankled to the stand-up counter where, uh oh, a different youngish dame was waiting to take orders. Though eager to talk to Sugar, he was hungry enough to eat a proverbial horse.

"I'll have a couple of Mystery Pies, with a bowl of fava beans on the side, no lettuce."

"Okay, but I have to warn you: Chef Algie has reserved all of his available Secret Sauce for a private function tomorrow night; and without the sauce, well, other customers have been ralphing today's pie."

"Ralphing?"

"Heaving, honking, hurling; shooting the cat. Call it what you like. Now, what do you want?"

What he wanted was to get his mitts on a jar of the Secret Sauce, but …No soap; and, "No one is allowed to bother Chef Algie," said the skirt, "not when he's cooking."

No way, José. He'd had only kibble biscuits for lunch, but…At a door signed *WARNING: Kitchen Intruders Are Fair Game!* Max stopped in his tracks as…

"Double, double, toil and trouble/ Something wicked this way comes!" someone in the cafe kitchen loudly chanted.

He pushed open the door and eased inside the kitchen. A youngish tall skinny guy, wearing one of those puffed-up chef's caps, was stooped over a large pot with a wooden-handled utensil in hand, stirring and…

"Eye of newt and toe of frog/ Wool of bat and tongue of dog/ In the cauldron boil and bake/ Fillet of a fenny snake."

With his appetite for a Mystery Pie doused in Secret Sauce somewhat waned, **"Yo!"** Max shouted.

The guy at the pot—Chef Algie, no doubt—looked up. Eyeing him like a wolf sizing up a goose, "No need to shout," said the cook. "You might curdle the sauce."

"Where's Sugar?"

"Sugar! Sugar! Sugar!" the oddball busted out chanting. **"When you wake up in the morning, feelin' kinda peckish/ This is often where you'll find her the most/ Livin' in your cereal, livin' in your yogurt, sometime even livin' in your toast."**

Max took a step back.

"Some people think that Sugar hangs out/ only with bright-colored cats/ But she spreads love all over your food/ and the company's been hidin' the facts/ Cola, granola, and pasta sauce/ mushy peas, mac-n-cheese, radish from a horse/ Fruit, and soup, even soup-in-a-satchel/ And muesli is Sugar they call all-natural."

"Hey, Buddy!" Max shouted just as loudly. Then in a lower voice, "All I want to know is where to find the chubby dame named Sugar who was working the front yesterday."

"I wouldn't know," said the wiseguy, peering into the pot; then looking up. "Last time I noticed, which could have been yesterday, she was perched—plump as a partridge—right there where you're standing, fat as a Christmas goose. Why do you ask?"

"Need to have a little chat about…Would you happen to have first-hand skinny on how Sugar and her stepmother get along?"

"Oh yeah, everybody knows that. They hated each other. That was the main thing we used to have in common."

Used to have in common? That and "hated each other" sounded like past tense.

"Johny, Johny/ Yes, Papah/ Eating sugar?/ No, Papah/ Open your mouth/ Ha! Ha! Ha!"

Hmmm? Max recalled O.B. Everheart saying his Missus and stepdaughter got along only so-so because Sugar was keeping company with a cook named Motley. The kid had also re-told that when the suspicious stepdaughter in *Case of Double Indemnity* got cozy with the insurance salesman, the wicked stepmother picked-up on the curveball in play and—plotting to make her first dead husband's daughter disappear—got cozy with the chick's sleazy boyfriend.

"Adder's fork and blind-worm's sting/ Lizard's leg and owlet's wing/ Fire burn and cauldron bubble…"

Max inched farther away from the crackpot. From back in his own junior high school days, *Case of Sweeney Todd: The Demon Barber of Fleet Street* came to mind. He had worked the curtains for an on-stage drama club musical production based on an old English case report about two murderous maniacs: a barber who cut the throats of customers, and an old broad who ground up the dead bodies and baked the remains in meat pies. Eyeballing the bubbling pot…beginning to feel sickish to his stomach… Max wondered if Chef Algie…

"Double, double, toil and trouble/ Like a hell-broth boil and bubble/ Cool it with a baboon's blood/ Then the charm is firm and good ♫

"Algie Motley!" someone semi-shouted. "Ten pounds of kava powder, at fifty dollars a pound? You'll have the guests in comas and us in the poorhouse!"

"Sauce for the gander, sauce for the goose, Mother."

The new more normal shouter was a shapely, easy-on-the-eyes middle-aged blonde who had rushed into the kitchen through a different door. Noticing that "fair game" had intruded, "Can't you read?! You could lose any or all of your digits in here when Algie's at work. And before you ask, the answer is no, we presently have not enough Secret Sauce cooked-up to share with cafe customers."

"Maximo Morrrgannn's the name. Private dicking is my game. Here to…"

"Private detective?!" the blonde said, with an alarmed look at the oddball chef. "Was that really just free-range roadkill the wranglers brought in this morning?"

"He's looking for Sugar, and spice and everything nice, Mother. Not filets of armadillo."

"Why?"

Feeling desperate to break the case before the hitchick and her pal got his number, "Just between us chickens and the lamppost for now," Max blurted, "Sugar's daddy is — to put gently — toes up."

"Toes up? Oh my God, that means…"

"Goosey goosey gander/ Whither shall I wander/ Upstairs and downstairs/ And in my lady's chamber…"

"O.B. Everheart's credit card will be rejected!" said the bossy broad. "Mimi will leave us holding an empty bag after tomorrow night's so-called investiture feast," she wailed, before turning and dashing from the kitchen.

"There I met an old man/ Who wouldn't say his prayers/ So I took him by his left leg/ And threw him down the stairs."

Max took off his fedora and scratched his bean. His intended play had been to get Sugar Everheart to bat her baby blues at Buford Bailey and turn the insurance salesman against her stepmother before the *femme fatale* plugged him, but now…

Hmmm. As a party to tomorrow night's investiture "Jubilee", Chef Algie Motley—no doubt Sugar Everheart's sleazy boyfriend—looked to already be in cahoots with the case's *femme fatale*, Mimi Everheart. And Sugar seemed to be on the lam, if not "in the soup", so to speak.

"Double, double, toil and trouble/ Something wicked this way comes."

THURSDAY

June 5, 2022

CHAPTER SIXTEEN

Fitfully sleeping, Mimi, imagined herself as back to being a child... *sitting on a sofa... Beside her, "Oh, goody, this was my dear mother's favorite one," said her own undear mother, as a man with slicked-back dark hair and a mustache appeared in black-and-white on a TV screen...*

"Do you want to be Queen for a Day?"...YESSSS!...

But now... back from her stumble at the Camelot Ball in London...Sugar, just born, stood full-grown beside her at a hospital bed..."Oh goody," said the old woman lying there, "chocolate-covered cherries are my favorite"...

"I know what you did," said the ever-resentful stepdaughter.

The picture on the TV screen turned to color...on the staircase landing at one end of Heraldry Hall, the mustachioed man, now wearing a red coat and hosting a new reality TV show, looked down at her ...With his swagger stick held over his head of slicked-back hair...

"Oo is the Rat in the Kitchen?"

Buzz. Buzz. Buzz.

Mimi woke with a start. She sat upright with a jerk. She rubbed sleep from her eyes. With a sigh of relief, she realized she had experienced only a nightmare and that this very night she would be crowned...

Buzz. Buzz. Buzz.

"Are you decent?" said the voice of Buford Bailey, again through both the phone she held to her ear and the bedroom door. "Mimi, we need to talk, face-to-face.

"Brace yourself, Mimi," said the overly attentive insurance agent as he entered her chamber. "To put it to you gently, well, it looks like O.B. met his Maker without a penny in his pocket to pay the piper."

"The old cheapskate never had cash on him."

"Your late husband was broke, Mimi. My sources at the bank told me, in strictest confidence, that O.B. has been spending like a drunk sailor. All the livestock have been auctioned off, the ranch mortgaged up to its gills, and this house too. Bottom line, there will be no inheritance for you to enjoy; only funeral expenses, if the remains are ever found."

Though shocked, "Thank goodness for the life insurance. Otherwise…"

"Well, uh, Mimi, I am sorry to have to tell you that an insurance pay-out is, well, up in the air. The company thinks suicide might be in play and…"

"Suicide! The 'company' thinks that selfish bastard shot himself in the ear while posing for a selfie, to selfishly keep me from getting double money?!"

"Well, yeah, that photo does present a wrinkle. I have instructed Chief Potter to drain Lake Henryetta and look for signs of foul play. I'm on your team, Mimi; pitching for murder."

"No, you idiot! It was death by accident. I am entitled to the 'double indemnity' pay-off you 'pitched for' at the cost of an arm-and-leg. That dumb fat detective can't prove it was murder. Get out of here, Buford, and do your job. Tell the company, no crime/ no nickel-and-dime."

As the ever-incompetent insurance agent scurried out the door, Mini collapsed onto her bed and closed her eyes, hoping she would fall asleep and awake to find that Buford Bailey's visitation had been only a part of an ongoing nightmare.

Instead, damnit, she tossed and turned; haunted by murky visions that she, like Hillary Clinton, would tragically wake to find that a vast right-wing conspiracy, so to speak, had somehow thwarted her rise to the high station in life to which she was entitled. No doubt her thoughtless ex-husband had in fact

posed for that photo, shot himself in the ear as a joke…but not fatally—definitely not fatally—before wandering off, perhaps to the shore of Lake Henryetta, and…

Hmmm? She wouldn't get way with it. Not this time, Sugar had said on the phone, obviously harkening back to her mother's death shortly following childbirth. What gall! Sugar herself was the murderess, for growing so fat in the womb, but of course blamed "the stepmother" to sugar-coat her guilt. And blamed her father too, no doubt. Oh yes, the not-so-sweet daughter resented O.B. for finding happiness in a second marriage.

Hmmm? Mimi again silently hmmmed. Other than she herself, who but Sugar would have thought they had a lot to gain by the demise of O.B. Everheart? Yes, the spoiled brat—second in line to get her hands on the old man's insurance money—must have shot her daddy in the ear, and took the photo with intent to pin the crime on the "wicked" widow. That was obviously why she had not gone to Tulsa as instructed, and…And had called on the phone to gloat that…no, to warn that she—her hated stepmother—would be next!

Mimi covered her head with a blanket.

Tap. Tap. Tap.

She buried herself deeper into the bedcovers.

"Are you decent, Madam?" said the voice—thank God—of Major Jesterson, come just in time to her rescue.

"Woke up to a rather imposing cock-up."

Cock-up?!

"Need you…"

Mimi threw off the bedding, rose from repose, stripped off her nightgown, and boldly rushed to the door.

CHAPTER SEVENTEEN

"No, I will not 'keep a stiff upper lip'," said Mamie to the persistent British woman, Vickers, who had barged into the Prairie Meats & Cafe management office and refused to leave. "We will not keep calm and carry on with a feast for Mimi Goodrich Everheart, no matter how much insurance money she is in line for. Her late husband's credit card was rejected. End of story."

"But to bail out at the eleventh hour under such regrettable circumstances; isn't that rather bad form on your part, Ms. Motley?"

"The 'rather bad form' is yours and your client's, thanks to which our little company is now faced with multiple 'sticky wickets', so to speak. Costs of more product than we have use for. Cancellation fees for other supplies and staff. And a pending special delivery of *foie gras*, for which a refund of almost ten thousand dollars is far from certain."

"*Foie gras*? No, under no circumstances would I, nor did I approve inclusion of that abominable French dish on the feast menu!"

Mamie braced herself for a gratuitous, self-righteous lecture against production, serving and consumption of the fatty ducks' livers that were the essential ingredients of Algie's so-called Secret Sauce.

Admittedly, she herself had at first been appalled by sight of her own son force-feeding ducks twice-a-day over three-week periods—a process called *gravage*—in order to enlarge their livers to ten times normal size. But Algie had educated her with

age-old truths underlying the not inhumane process dating back five thousand years.

Neither ducks nor geese had a gagging reflex. They had no teeth for chewing; swallowed food and even rocks whole down industrial-strength esophaguses unsusceptible to pain. And whereas ducks sold in markets and restaurants were slaughtered after five or six weeks of typically caged existence, *foie gras* donors enjoyed a full twelve weeks of free-range life before *gravage* began. The end product—called by Anthony Bourdain "one of the ten most important flavors in gastronomy"-- was universally acclaimed to be delicious. Nevertheless, some people…

"As I made perfectly crystal to Chef Algernon, the major would rather die than be associated with the serving anything French in nature. He cannot abide the Frogs."

Let livers live free, or die! …Let livers live free, or die!…Let livers live free, or…

Loud shouting came, not from the lips of Ms. Vickers nor from the kitchen.

Friends don't eat friends!…Friends don't eat friends!… Friends don't eat friends!… Friends don't eat…

Mamie dashed from the office, through the cafe and into the parking lot, where dozens of people had assembled and more were arriving; all chanting and/ or brandishing stick-mounted signs…**LIVERS ARE TORTURE VICTIMS!…CRUELTY IS NO DELICACY!…STOP GRAVAGE!…**

Algie came to her side—apparently from the skinning-and-butchering room—his apron covered in blood, a large butcher knife in hand.

Friends don't eat friends!…Friends don't torture livers!… Stop gravage! Stop gravage! Stop gravage!

Some of the protesters were in costumes of sorts, including a man—also wearing a bloody apron as well as a wire-mesh face mask—who came up to Algie and hissed: "I think I'll eat <u>your</u> liver, along with some fava beans and a nice bottle of chianti."

Bite back for animals! …Bite back for animals!… Bite back for animals!… Bite back…

The masked man aggressively stepped closer, but…

"I'm Slim Shady, yeah, I'm the real Shady" Algie loudly chanted. **"We ain't nothin' but mammals/ Well, some of us, cannibals/ Who cut people open like cantaloupes…"**

The masked man took a tentative step backward.

"Algie! Stop it! Give me the knife."

"Chill out, man" said the other man, backing away. "You've got a screw loose in your head."

Friends don't eat friends!…Don't treat animals like animals!… Friends don't eat animals!… Don't eat…

The angry chanting suddenly stopped. A stoutish woman in military-like clothes—wearing also what looked to be possibly a Mother Goose mask—emerged from the crowd . Three little children—costumed as ducks—followed her toward Algie; loudly singing:

♪Be kind to our web-footed friends/ For a duck may be somebody's mother/ Be kind to our friends in the swamp/ Where the weather is very, very damp/ Well, you may think this is the end… ♫

"But it's not," said Algie to "Mother Goose".

Friends don't eat friends!… Friends don't eat friends!… Friends…

"This little piggy went to market," said her son in a normal tone of voice, pointing to one of the little girls. "This little piggy stayed home," he said, pointing to another little girl. "And this little piggy went wee, wee, wee/ **As she ran away from the farmer's wife/ Who cut off her head with a carving knife!"**

Ohhhhh… the crowd moaned.

"How dare you threaten these children, you bloodthirsty brute!" said the woman, ripping off her mask. "As an officer in the Animal Rights Militia, I brought these three little girls here to peacefully protest torture of ducks for production of that disgusting *foie gras* this cafe puts on everything!"

In a startling flash, Mamie wondered: How did the protesters know *foie gras* was the main ingredient of Algie's Secret Sauce?

"You needn't have worried your own silly head, Mother Goose," said Algie. "Only fully grown male ducks are required to sacrifice their livers for mankind's nourishment."

"That's good to hear. White males of all species deserve…"

"Immediately after hatching, adorable little female duckings are put in meat grinders and made into cat food."

Ohhhhhh…

"Three little kittens lost their mittens," Algie then shouted above the heads of the three little girls, who had shed their duck masks and begun to cry. **"Meow, meow, meow/ Oh Mommy, dear, she here, see here, our mittens we have lost/ What! Lost your mittens?/ You naughty kittens/ You shall have no pie/ And they all ran away from the farmer's wife/ who cut off their heads…"**

Ohhhhhh…

Oh no. Mamie cringed as a large FedEx truck…

Honk. Honk. Honk.

…pulled into the parking lot and slowly made its way through the crowd.

Booooooooooo…

The driver, after setting up a ramp and going into the back of the truck, rolled out a dolly laden with…Oh no again; in addition to *THREE MUSKETEERS, Purveyors of Foie Gras and Other Delicacies* painted on a large barrel, which was bad enough, also painted on the container was a cartoon-like illustration of three smiling white ducks waddling across a lush green field toward a sparkling blue pond.

LET LIVERS LIVE FREE, OR DIE! the mob as one roared, before pouncing on the delivery man and…Mamie gasped, as the barrel lid came off, spilling almost ten thousand dollars worth of product onto the parking lot pavement.

Like starving ants, the protestors set upon the pricey flash-frozen packets as though they were proverbial popsicles dropped on a sidewalk by a terrified Good Humor Man and…Away the duck liver lovers scurried in all directions.

With Algie still at her side, Mamie ran to the meager scattered remains and—ignoring the delivery man's complaints—scooped up what was left.

"Oh well," said her son, who had stubbornly refused to accept the prior necessity of canceling the feast. "Loaves and fishes, Mother, loaves and fishes. We'll somehow make do."

With a sigh, Mamie walked toward Ms. Vickers, standing on the edge of the parking lot with mouth agape.

"Not to worry," she said to the British woman. "Our upper lips are now stiff as boards for remaining calm and carrying on."

"Good show!"

Back inside her office, Mamie collapsed into a chair, put her elbows on the desk, and leaned her drooping head into her hands. In truth, she could not imagine how they could possibly carry on without an adequate supply of *foie gras* for Secret Sauce. The only consolation to the debacle she could think of was that celebration of Mimi's "investiture" would be...

Hmmm. Though militant groups such as the Animal Rights Militia were known to routinely track and harass deliveries from the *Three Musketeers* duck ranch in New Jersey, Mamie again wondered how the ARM protesters had known that *foie gras* was the essence of Secret Sauce.

Hmmm. She now recalled Algie telling her that Sugar Everheart hated Mimi as much as she herself despised the bitch. On that basis, she had muted her objection to the girl hanging around. But now...

Hmmm. It occurred to Mamie that Sugar might well have tipped off the mob—not necessarily with intent to undermine Algie's venture—but in an attempt to sabotage her stepmother's big night.

Hmmm.

CHAPTER EIGHTEEN

Knock. Knock-Knock. Knock.

Max, already anxiously waiting inside the back door, held his breath.

Knock. Knock-Knock. Knock…**Knock! Knock!**

Max opened the door. In rushed the kid, carrying two paper sacks.

"Sorry for the delay, Mr. Maximo," he said, putting the sacks on the kitchen table. "After buying out Burger King's first round of cheeseburgers, I had to tap into Dairy Queen."

Max dug into the sack labeled *Dairy Queen*.

"In answer to what you must be wondering, Mr. Max, the answer is still no. Still no report that the client's body has been found, or even any chatter that poor old Mr. Everheart bought the farm. But Mr. Quickie said cops were seen out at Lake Henryetta, and might have been dredging."

Yeah, just like the the local flatfoots under Potter's command: a day late and a dollar short.

"A dame—must have been that English speaking skirt you pegged as a hitchick—was at the copy shop counter," said the kid, slapping a couple of printed cards on the table. "She comped Mr. Quickie this pair of invitations to tonight's Festive Rites of Investiture at the Everheart mansion. But it seems Mrs. Quickie is a picky eater, so the Mister passed them on to us."

Max almost gagged at the thought of attending the rites catered by that Prairie Home Cafe chef.

"The investiture is not for the *femme fatale's* marital dead-meat, Mr. Maximo. According to Mr. Quickie, the festive rites

are to celebrate Mrs. Everheart's entry into a religious Order of a Virgin Cecilia. So you know what that means."

Yeah, same old story: the black widow had come down with a guilty conscience. Now the deadly dame was going to try praying her way out of a murrrderrr rap.

"Nuns are required to live lives of poverty and chastity, Mr. Maximo, so Mrs. Everheart would not have had motive to rub out her spouse when she set up the investiture, which must have happened well before her husband's permanent disappearance."

"Yeah, the case is a can of worms alright," said Max, putting down a burger. "Turns out the victim's daughter's boyfriend—an oddball cook named Algie—was already in cahoots with the *femme fatale* by the time I made my play. And Sugar was…For crying out loud, the blonde broad behind the racket of selling the sleazy boyfriend's meat pies to unsuspecting customers flashed O.B. Everheart's credit card right in front of me, wailing that dead men are deadbeats."

"We should track down the daughter, and…"

"She's in the wind, or maybe in the…Trust me, kid, we don't want to know where Sugar might be."

"Hmmm," the kid hmmmed. "This is starting to sound like a same old story. Ever wonder how Cinderella happened to be a stepdaughter in the Olde English fairytale?"

"No, and I still don't care."

"In the Italian first part of the story called *Cenerentola*, a supposedly kind and caring governess convinced Cinderella to kill a prior stepmother so she—the governess—could marry the rich father. But then the broad had ugly daughters of her own. That's the back story. Cinderella a/k/a Cenerentola deserved the treatment she got from her wicked stepmother."

Except for the ones about Little Jack Horner and Georgy Porgy, Max had never been interested in children's stories.

"Hmmm," the kid again hmmmed. "We may be dealing, not with a replay of *Case of Double Indemnity*, but with a replay of *Case of the Fall River Legend*."

As Max went back to munching burgers, the kid went way back to a pre-*Noir* case involving a stepdaughter named Lizzie Borden:

According to numerous books and film documentaries, the New England skirt had disliked a stepmother she suspected of marrying her wealthy widowed father for his money; and equally disliked her daddy, not only for enriching the stepmother at her expense, but also for killing a bunch of pigeons she had built a barn roost for. After the parents' deaths within the same hour, it turned out that members of the household had been sickened the week before, and that Lizzie had bought a bottle of poison at the local drugstore. She herself discovered both bodies, and was overheard by a housemaid minutes later, laughing.

"The case got a lot of national attention," said the kid. "Heck, to the tune of an old song called *Ta-Ra-Ra Boom De-Ay*, young schoolgirls skipped rope and sang:

♫Lizzie Borden took an axe/ and gave her mother forty whacks/ When she saw what she had done/ she gave her father forty-one♫

"An axe murderess?" Max was sickened to imagine the gory details.

"And almost a hundred years later, a song titled *Lizzie Borden* reached #44 on a *Billboard* Hot 100 chart."

♫You can't chop up your Papa in Massachusetts/ not even if it's planned as a surprise/ No, you can't chop up your Papa in Massachusetts/ You know how neighbors criticize♫

Max eyed a half-eaten burger for a moment; then dropped it onto the table, as the kid went on singing:

♫You can't chop up your Mama in Massachusetts/ not even if you're tired of her cuisine/ No, you can't chop up your Mama in Massachusetts/ You know it's sure to cause a scene♫

Max began to get the drift—could be that Sugar Everheart, not her stepmother, was in cahoots with the modern-day "Barber of Fleet Street" at the Prairie Home Cafe—and then the kid went on to over-egg the pudding.

♫She never did the slightest thing/ that Mom and Papa bid/ They said, Lizzie, cut it out/ So that's exactly what she did ♫

Though still in Mom's doghouse and underfed, Max pushed both sacks of the remaining uneaten burgers-and-fries away from him.

"Lizzie Borden was put on trial but skated, Mr. Maximo, with an inheritance that today would be worth multi-millions. You know what that means."

"Spell it out for me."

"It means we have to use these comped ducats to get into the Everheart mansion. We need to stop Sugar Everheart from offing her stepmother. The Missus is the client's widow, after all. And the invitation says there will be an all-you-can-eat Olde English buffet."

Max got up from the table, hot-footed to a bathroom off a hallway, dropped to his knees and commenced to heave, to hurl, to honk, and…Further imagining an all-you-can-eat Olde English buffet catered by Chef Algie, shot the remains of possibly a cat named Ralph into what sailors called "the can".

CHAPTER NINETEEN

From her post at the repeatedly opening-and-closing door leading from the Everheart mansion kitchen to the off-limits banquet hall, Mamie could only listen, wonder and worry about what trouble was afoot.

Local yokels, ever susceptible to advertisement of anything "free"—and no doubt understandably curious—had begun arriving for Mimi's "festive rites of investiture" two hours earlier than invited. Algie had nevertheless ordered the wranglers—"liveried" in borrowed black-and-white high school band uniforms—to serve wine, whiskey, ale, cider and mead to the thirsty mob.

Minstrels, mummers and other hired acts had also been sent in to raucously entertain. For the past two hours, merrymakers…

♫**From France we do get brandy, from Jamaica comes the rum/ But stout beer and strong cider are in Jolly Olde England's…**♫

Seeming strangely calm while stirring a large pot of Secret Sauce—watered down with extra portions of Madeira—her red-eyed, obviously exhausted son now joined in loudly singing:

♫**So give me the punch ladle, and I'll fathom the bowl/ I'll fathom the bowl, I'll fathom the bowl/ Give me the punch ladle and I'll fathom the bowl…**♫

As the guests in the so-called "Hall of Heraldry" continued singing the Olde English drinking song's chorus, "Not to worry, Mother," said Algie, holding up a spritzer bottle in his other hand. "A mist of modified Secret Sauce is good as a mile of…"

♫**An old man, he do lie in the cold depths of the sea/ No stone at his head, but what matters that to he?/ There's a clear, crystal fountain in Jolly Olde England shall roll/ So give me the punch ladle, and I'll fathom the bowl** ♫

♫**I'll fathom the bowl, I'll fathom the bowl…** ♫

"The beast needs food in its belly, Algie!" one of the wranglers semi-shouted as he came into the kitchen with a gust of noise. "The whole damn bunch are already drunk as a skunks."

"O, Oysters come and walk with us,'" Algie shouted. **"'The time has come to talk of many things/ Of shoes — and ships — and sealing wax/ and of cabbages — and kings/ And why the sea is boiling hot/ And whether pigs have wings.'"**

After wranglers had brought platters of bloody Prairie "Oysters" past him for misting, her son turned to her and again said, "Not to worry, Mother." He then smiled wickedly, and added: "I have added a tad more *Poivre des Cannibales* to the Secret Sauce mix, which should excuse overdone rawness."

Uh oh. Intending only too add a tad of minor mischief to Mimi's affair, Mamie herself had already added extra *Poivre des Cannibales* — another term for powdered kava — to the pot of Secret Sauce. But too much of the intoxicating long pepper extract, especially when combined with consumption of alcohol, could cause not only harmless cases of diarrhea among guests; it could cause their livers to burst.

"Sauce for the gander, sauce for the goose," Algie said, with a wink. "Plenty of porta-pots and barf bowls on hand."

In need of a breath of air not tinged with the heady aroma of peppered *foie gras*, Mamie walked across the kitchen and through a doorway into a stairwell connected to the mansion's second floor. Sensing a presence in the dimly lit space, she wheeled around and…*deja vu* all over again.

The tall man's slicked-back hair was thinnish, and a mustache was new, but…"Larry?"

"Lawrence Jamieson a/k/a Major Lawrence Jesterton, at your service, Miss Motley," said the red-coated hotel waiter from her past life. "Donkey's years, Mamie, what?"

"'Major Jesterson' is it? Now officer of an 'Escoffier Brigade'? What on earth are you up to, Larry?"

"'Appened to spot a posting for 'ere in 'Enryetta. Thought I might catch a glimpse. Never expected you and the lad would be catering the affair. Chip off the old block, what?"

She didn't dare ask if father-and-son were in cahoots.

"Married now, are we?" he asked.

"Not I. Still couldn't say about 'we'."

"Trouble-and-strife left me, Mamie. I'm fancy free."

"So is Mimi Goodrich, as it 'appens'."

"'So I 'ear. And the Madam was also an American cheese deb, so they say."

"Soon to become a British Baroness, and a virgin to boot, so they also now say."

"Ah, Mamie: cheeky as ever, and still attractively top-'eavy, I must say."

"Ah, Larry: still unattractively full of yourself and a ton of bullshit, I must say."

And that was that. After silently sizing-up each other for a few more seconds, they parted; he up the stairs, no doubt bound for Mimi's bedroom; she back into the kitchen. How ironic if Mimi Goodrich, of all people, were to become "trouble-and-strife" of the hotel waiter she had once—sight unseen—so viciously looked down on.

Inside the kitchen, Mamie noticed two entertainers huddled beside the door to the banquet hall: one costumed as perhaps Cinderella, the other black-robed and propped with a scythe as the Grim Reaper. As she approached, they seemed to be arguing, but then… into the now rowdier hall went "Death".

♪**My man, he do not disturb me when I'm laid at my ease/ He does as he likes and he says as he please/ That man, he's the devil, he's black as the coal/ So give me the ladle, and I'll fathom the bowl…** ♫

After lingering at the opened doorway for a few moments, "Cinderella" turned around, took off a pig mask and—holding in her hand a container of powdered kava—said:

"Oh! Mrs. Motley; so sorry to have bailed without notice. My father took deathly sick while visiting a, uh, an associate. Cowboys came and helped me take Daddy out to his ranch, which had always been his chosen resting place."

As Sugar Everheart put her hand holding the kava container behind her back, Mamie visually scanned the kitchen, but… Algie was nowhere to be seen.

♫**I'll fathom the bowl, I'll fathom the bowl/ Give me the punch ladle/ and I'll fathom the bowl** ♫

CHAPTER TWENTY

♫I was beat, incomplete/ I'd been had, I was one of a batch/ But you made me feel/ Yeah, you made me feel like a catch…♫

As one of the many tasteless so-called parodies of Madonna's classic song forced itself through her head, Mimi—dressed in the virginal white nightgown required for her impending investiture—paced from one draped window of her bedroom toward another. She was tired of being a "virgin", and beginning to have doubts about Major Jesterson. For crying out loud, yesterday he dropped Diana's wine glass on the grand apple-and-pearscase. He had not attended dinner later, nor had he tapped on her bedroom door until this morning, with a "cock-up" that turned out to be only a hiccup about "feast financing".

♫I was freezing, I was on ice/ But you thawed me out, you wanted a slice/ You thawed me out/ Yes, your love thawed me out/ Like a sturgeon…♫

At a table beneath the draped window, she re-filled the now stemless wine glass with an Olde English beverage called mead, turned around and paced back toward the other draped window. She was even having doubts—and fears—about going through with local investiture rites of becoming the Virgin Baroness of Bridgewater Abbey.

Feast-and-frolic had been going on in Heraldry Hall for hours and, to judge by the racket, the festivities were getting rowdier and rowdier. On her knees in front of the major on the Hall's staircase landing, she would be a kneeling duck for Sugar and that horrid, no doubt also vengeful Motley boy.

♫*I wasn't newish, I had already been caught/ but you, you weren't Jewish, about scales I had not / Yeah, you took a slice before I started to rot/ Like a sturgeon…* ♫

Mimi veered to the door of the mistress suite, unlatched a chain, opened the door a crack and…. Oh no, the major's armed batman, Bates, had abandoned his assigned post!

Mimi gulped a mouthful of mead.

Maybe her bodyguard had relocated to a more advantageous spot, she hoped, tiptoeing from the suite and down the hall, where…

♫**We hunted all day, my boys, but nothing we could find/ But a porcupine in a field, and him we left behind…** ♫

…from a balcony overlooking Heraldry Hall, she saw no one standing on the stairway landing, but. . .

♫**The Englishman said, a porcupine, the Scotsman he said, nay/ The Irishman said, it's a pincushion, with pins stuck in the wrong way!** ♫

…at the foot of the stairs, that fat detective, her only protection from an attack by Sugar and Mamie Motley's bastard son… Oh no, he too now hurried from his post.

♫**Then fill each glass and let it pass/ No sign of care betray/ We will drink and sing while the bells do ring/ All on Saint David's day!** ♫

An intoxicating aroma rose in the air, but…in the grand saloon below…Ugh. Mimi's knees almost buckled at sight of disgusting dead meat piled on the long Hall table… hordes of common riff-raff plonked side-by-side on benches…eating the bloody carrion with their hands…drinking from large cans… loudly roaring…

♫**We hunted all the day, my boys, but nothing we could find/ But a natterjack toad in an open field, and him we left behind…** ♫

And now uniformed members of the local high school band were bringing to the table…OMG!… a whole fatted sheep on a spit, dripping grease by the gallon…roasted whole whole fowl of some kind. . . pigs' heads with the tops sawed off, spilling gray

mush onto platters…live creatures leaping like frogs from large pots of boiling oil…

♫The Englishman said, a toad, the Scotsman he said, nay/ The Irishman said, it's grandma's duck with the feathers all blown away♫

Costumed guitar and tambourine players egged the mob on… Someone dressed like Robin Hood clumsily juggled in the smoky air, and repeatedly dropped raw eggs…Dancers wearing animal face masks pranced about…

♫We hunted all the day, my boys, but nothing we could find/ But a great black pig in a field, and him we left behind… ♫

Flaming torches filled the Hall with sooty smoke and… OMG!…Lined up against the side walls… her collection of family crests were obscured by…by dozens of portable toilets!

♫The Englishman said, a black pig, the Scotsman he said, nay/ Poor Paddy said, it's the devil himself, so we all three ran away! ♫

Mimi dropped the stemless wine glass, leaned over the balcony rail, tossed her cookies, so to speak, and…In terror, she fled back toward the mansion's mistress suite, chased by the sound of…

♫Then fill each glass and let it pass/ No sign of care betray/ We will drink and sing while the bells do ring… ♫

Inside her bedroom, she dashed to her bed and covered her head. For awhile all was quiet, but then…

"'Ark, 'ark!/ The watch-dogs bark!/ 'Ark, ark! you 'ear/ The strain of a strutting chanticleer/ Cock-a-doodle-dooo.'"

Mimi shrank in dread as the door came open and…There stood Major Jesterson, holding what looked to be a bottle of champagne.

"Bout to pop my own cork," he said and…*Pop!*… "out comes the weasel."

Her hour of doom had come, she thought. Like Joan of Arc, also a virgin, she would march down the grand staircase. Sugar would be lurking, likely armed with a flagon of poison, the usual wily female way. Or that boyfriend of hers—a common

cook who once bit the head off a live pigeon in front of a prom queen—might push her into a pot of…

"No need to 'urry," said the major, sitting down on the bed and loosening his red coat. "And no need to wait neither. I could close the Queen's eyes, put fingers in 'er ears, and 'Er Majesty would be none the wiser about status of your 'maydenhede'."

Noticing that his "weasel" had indeed popped out of his trousers, in a matter of seconds, Mimi had her suitor lying naked on her bed; her virginal nightgown lying crumpled on the floor, and…It had been awhile, a very long while, but everyone said "doing it" was like riding a bicycle. On top and peddling, so to speak, uh oh…a tire, so to speak, went flat.

"On second thought," said the major. "In wise words of the Bard: 'If I broke your virgin knot/ Before sanctimonious full and 'oly rites were ministered/ You would 'ate me/ Therefor take 'eed as…'"

"Close your eyes and put fingers back in your ears," she insisted, but…

"No, Madam, I cannot let your charms melt my honor into lust/ To take away the edge of tonight's celebration."

Mimi went back to "peddling" with increased vigor, but…

"No, no, no," the major wailed. "'The white cold virgin snow upon my 'eart/ Abates the ardor of my liver.'"

Mimi sighed. Qualifying for an upper-class title was proving to be more complicated…and frustrating…not to mention more dangerous than she had imagined, but…Again she sighed. Once the rites of investiture were—God willing—survived, with a re-inflated Baron Jesterson at her side—and occasionally under her—the reward would be worth all the toil and trouble.

CHAPTER TWENTY-ONE

Returned from being hounded out of a porta-pot, Max again stood guard at the foot of a grand staircase anchoring one end of an Everheart mansion room, big and loud as a high school gymnasium during a pep rally.

♫**John Adams lies here, of the parish of Southwell/ A carrier who carried the can to his mouth quite well...** ♫

The kid was supposed to be backing him up, but had been turned away at the door because booze was being served.

♫**He carried so much, and he carried so fast/ He could carry no more, and was carried at last...** ♫

Still, if Sugar Everheart made a play to get at her stepmother in private, she would have to go through almost two hundred and fifty pounds of, okay, not muscle but that much lard would at least slow the dame down.

♫**For the liquor he drank, being too much for one/ He could not carry off, so he's now carri-on!**

Along sides of a long table loaded down with meats, guests continued to feed like hogs at a trough, drink like already drunk sailors, and bellow...also like drunk sailors.

Ha, Ha, Ha, Ha, Ha, Ha...

Most of the merrymakers had barfed onto the floor and table. Others were inside, or banging doors to get inside porta-pots lining the hall. Some seemed to have given up waiting. A few had keeled over onto the filthy floor.

Ha, Ha, Ha, Ha, Ha, Ha...

To Max the Olde English Feast was unappetizing, and yet... Aromatic hints of Chef Algie's Secret Sauce in the smoky air

tempted him to…No, a fleeting image of O.B. Everheart's remains being ground up in the Prairie Home Cafe kitchen warded off an urge to take a bite or two out of one or two of the Mystery Meat Pies littering the table.

The oddball chef—at last check—was in the kitchen, loudly chanting "up comes the first one, up comes the second one/ Oh how they wiggle and squirm" like a madman.

Sugar was not *en fragrante*, but possibly *en cognito* as a masked member of a troupe of entertainers, one of which—unmasked except for a red rubber nose—now jumped up onto the table with a bullhorn in hand.

"A panhandler outside the hall said he hadn't had a bite in days," the joker bellowed, **"so I bit him!"**

Ha, Ha, Ha…

"My wife is such a bad cook we say prayers <u>after</u> meals."

Ha, Ha, Ha…

"Speaking of food, wanna know why the cannibal king threw up after eating the court jester?"

Ha, Ha, Ha…

"The comic didn't taste funny."

Max laughed out loud, but otherwise…crickets.

"I mean, he <u>did</u> taste funny!

Booooooo…

"Take my wife, please take my wife."

Boooooooooo…

Under a barrage of bloody meat that looked to be mainly raw livers, the comedian jumped off the stage. In his place came the red-coated waiter who had attended to Mimi Everheart in the flower garden yesterday.

"Your attention, please; may I 'ave your attention, please," he bellowed through a bullhorn.**"To start the formal ceremony, 'ere tonight—direct from opera 'alls of Old Blighty, by way of St. Louis—we 'ave on 'and Miss Pigathia Lee, to render the Olde English song you Yanks borrowed for your national anthem."**

A few in attendance managed to get to their feet and, like Max, sing along for a few verses, but…Halfway through, he realized the words being rendered by the fat lady standing on the table made no sense.

♫…**I'll lend you my name and inspire you, to boot/ And besides I'll instruct you, like me, to intwine…** ♫

Booooooooo…

Bones and fava beans rained down on the opera singer, but still…

♫**While thus we agree, our toast let it be/ May we flourish happy, united and free/ And long may the Sons of Anacreon intwine/ with the myrtle of Venus and Bacchus's vine!** ♫

Booooooooooooooo…

Max swiveled his head, looked up, and…From upper steps of the staircase, Mimi Everheart, wearing a white nightgown—looking confused and wobbly—started down.

Booooooooooooooooooo…

On the staircase landing, uh oh…**Ohhhhhh**, the mob moaned, as the Widow Everheart collapsed onto her knees and…. **Ohhhhhh,** they again moaned, as she looked around, then tapped herself on the nose with a finger and…**Ohhhhh**… up on her feet she rose.

♫**The master, the swabber, the boatswain and I/ The gunner and his mate/ Loved Moll, Meg, and Margery/ But none of us cared for Kate ..** ♫

As a group of young dames wearing red choir robes clustered at the foot of the stairs, the nun-to-be—looking more confused and wobblier—continued her descent into the hall.

♫**For Kate had a tongue with a tang/ Would cry to a sailor, Go hang…** ♫

Though behind the red-robed group, the red-coated yardbird—still standing on the table—waved a bandleader's leather-covered stick and…

Uh oh, across the room Chef Algie came through a door from the kitchen, carrying a jumbo-size pie — possibly laced with an

explosive substance, or worse—with what must have been fifty lit candles stuck in it. Max reached for Old Junior.

♫**Happy Birthday to you**♫ the red-robed choir sang. ♫**Happy Birthday to you/ Happy Birthday Baroness Goodrich/ Happy Birthday…** ♫

Uh oh again. Another entertainer—wearing a black robe and carrying a bladed farming tool—pushed his or her way through the singers and…. With the bozo's back to him, Max was able to see only the shocked look on Mimi Everheart's face as she looked up into the masked farmer's eyes a split second before…

"You!" she said, before falling to the floor like a cut-down weed.

♫**Yea, Kate had a tongue with a tang…** ♫

By the time Max pushed through the crowd, the victim seemed to have recovered from only momentarily fainting in the face of possibly only an apparent attack. Lying in the muck, looking more bewildered than before, "Shut your eyes and ears, damnit!" she said, to the red-coated waiter who had got to her first. "I am still entitled to be titled. I was born to be a Virgin Baroness."

Max ripped a skeleton mask off the black-robed attacker, but… Instead of confronting Sugar Everheart…What the Sam Hill?…He came face-to-face with none other than his client, O.B. Everheart!

"Sorry to have ducked you, podner," the old man said with a grin. "Sugar came by and took me out to the ranch, but…Well, I just couldn't miss the party," he said with a wider grin. "Didn't have the cash to make Mimi a Queen for a Day. It cost me all I had left to answer that Peerage Society of England magazine ad for her to become a titled Baroness. But I sure enough made Mimi happy, didn't I."

♫**She loved not the savor of tar nor of pitch/ Yet a tailor might scratch her where she had the itch/ Then to sea, boys, and let Katy go hang!** ♫

In view of the unexpected turn of events, Max ankled over to the table and…Hmmm. Smelled like fish; tasted like liver.

Gosh, those Olde English meat pies doused with Secret Sauce
were good.

THE
END